THE FABRIC OVER THE MOON

Copyright © 2021 by Ferran Plana

First paperback edition October 2021

Book design by Nuno Moreira, NMDESIGN.ORG

ISBN 9798485883867

28 short stories from
unlikely heroes

THE FABRIC OVER THE MOON

Ferran Plana

TABLE OF CONTENTS

IZAH

When Mary Jane visited my village, she was astonished. It was not for our communal wooden huts where four or five families resided together, neither for the fact of living in the middle of the forest isolated from the rest of the world. It was our traditions that shocked her the most.

We met for the first time in the hardware store when I went to buy stuff we needed for repairing some of our huts after the huge storm of November 1971. She stared at me with an inquisitive face, probably wondering if my clothing was a costume. I wore my bison trousers and a simple skunk hat. We were used to being observed by the outsiders when we were out of the forest. Her face was so dazzling and delicate it captivated me. She caught my eyes and came to me.

"Nice outfit," she said, "it looks so pretty."

"Thank you."

"Are you going to any kind of contest...or party?"

"No, not really..."

"I have never seen you around. Are you new in town?" she asked.

"Well, I'm not from here, but I live very close."

"Ah, are you from Susanville?"

"No," I said, "I'm from Izah."

"Izah? Never heard of it. Anyway, my name is Mary Jane."

"Nice to meet you, Mary Jane. I am Brody."

She invited me to get a coffee in a cafe next to the store. We chatted for about two hours. I explained that I lived in a village in the forest called Izah. We didn't follow the rules and the laws from the outsiders, and we would only leave our village for necessary matters. She looked fascinated by our community. I felt overwhelmed; it was the first time I had such a long conversation with an outsider. She gave me her address in case I wanted to send a letter to her or visit her.

It took three months until there was a need to go out of the village again. The winter was very cold, and we were running out of groceries. I volunteered to go to town in order to buy cereal. Nobody complained.

I bounced to Mary Jane's house and stepped inside. It was a tiny house with very little furniture, and the smell of fresh baked cake whetted my appetite. Mary Jane was in the kitchen. She hadn't notice me until I said hello, to which she leaped and emitted a loud yelp.

"Don't you know how to knock before coming in?"

"I'm sorry... I thought that I was invited to enter when you gave me your address."

She prepared two cups of tea and offered the sofa for me to sit on. It was so soft and comfortable; I was used to sitting on wooden chairs. She explained to me that she lived with her aunt in this house, and she worked in a bar. I had seen bars, but I had never been inside any.

"I want you to come to Izah," I said.

"I would love to!" she said with a smile. "Is it far?"

"About five hours by walk."

"When could I visit you?"

"You can come with me today."

"Today? But it's late...and I have work tomorrow."

"You can stay in my hut."

"You know what? Fuck it. I'm coming with you."

We bought plenty of cereal from the grocery store. She insisted on helping me carry the food. The trek to Izah was hard for Mary Jane, she pleaded for a break five times, but she never lost her smile.

We reached Izah when it was already dark. The mist and dimness was broken by the glow of the small torches standing outside the huts. There were still some villagers outdoors, peering at Mary Jane suspiciously.

"Why are they all looking at me with those eyes?" she asked.

"We don't have a lot of outsiders visiting us. Actually, the last one I can remember came here about nine years ago. I was a child. He left after two weeks."

"What happened to him?"

"I don't know. He vanished."

I walked Mary Jane to my hut. The brief light from the central fireplace revealed all the inhabitants of the house. At the moment, in my hut resided four families, ten people in total. I introduced her to my mother.

"Mother, this is Mary Jane."

She smiled. "Welcome, Mary Jane."

"Nice to meet you."

"Tomorrow we will do the welcoming ceremony," said my mother. "Now you can go to sleep and rest."

We lay on the wool mattress with Mary Jane under the same blanket made from buffalo skin. She looked concerned.

"What is the welcoming ceremony? Why didn't you mention it to me?" she asked.

"I forgot about it. But don't worry, it's just a simple symbolic act we do for newborns and outsiders. Let's rest, Mary Jane."

"Goodnight."

I opened my eyes in the night. Mary Jane was holding my hand firmly, moving it around, and she stared at me with huge eyes. A din of moans and gasps coming from inside our hut was clearly audible. She pointed at the center of the hut where next to the fireplace lay two silhouettes shivering together. Some of the inhabitants of the hut sat in their blankets observing them.

"Are they having sex?" she asked.

"Yes. It's nighttime. They are aroused, and they will have a child. Do you want to watch them from closer?"

"What? No! This should be an intimate act!"

She turned her head and closed her eyes. I didn't understand her reaction until later on, when she explained to me that outsiders didn't have sex in front of other people, and they didn't believe that the attention of others during sexual intercourse would make them more fertile.

We woke up on a sunny and cold winter day. I took Mary Jane on a walk through the village before her welcoming ceremony. She was stupefied by how big Izah was, repeating several times the peaceful feeling she had while passing through the wooden huts, pacing on the paths ringed by colorful flowers and dense trees and hearing the chirp of the birds. She had fun observing the villagers, pointing out our clothes made from animal skins.

A blast resonated from the other side of the village. All the people left what they were doing and headed in the direction of the sound.

"The welcoming ceremony," I said to Mary Jane.

"I hope it doesn't consist of human sacrifice," she said.

Mary Jane tittered. I guided her to the ceremony stone while she was holding my hand strongly. The ceremony stone was a huge, round, flat rock, a kind of altar placed on the edge of the village with no huts close to it, just trees. Everybody was already waiting in absolute silence. I helped her climb onto the stone. She looked jittery.

"Take off your clothes," I said.

"What?"

"You have to take off your clothes now."

"In front of everybody? Are you crazy?"

"Don't worry, we will provide you with a good bison dress after, so you won't be cold. The ceremony will only last a few minutes."

Mary Jane glanced at the villagers that waited. She undressed timidly and threw her clothes on the icy grass. She looked even more gorgeous without her outsider clothes.

The ceremony started. The oldest woman of the village went up on the stone. She examined Mary Jane from up close, smelling her from head to toe without touching her, and got off the stone in silence. One by one, all the villagers stepped on the stone and observed and smelled Mary Jane. Her face changed as the villagers passed. In the beginning, she looked tense, staring at me with frightened eyes and trying to cover her body with her arms. Later, she became more relaxed, she released her arms and adopted a more comfortable position. I was the last one in the ceremony. I went up and admired her body from up close. Her skin had goosebumps, but she didn't look cold. Her smell was fresh and evoked a scent of pinecone and grass, inspiring the spirit of a good heart and a free soul. Our eyes made contact, and she gave me a sincere smile.

The ceremony finished, and the oldest woman from the village gave her a stunning bison dress and a raccoon hat. Mary Jane and I sat next to the ceremony stone where the sun warmed our skin.

"Thank you for the dress, it's so warm."

"Welcome to Izah!" I said.

"I didn't expect this kind of action," she said. "It was... How can I say it? Weird?"

"We celebrate this ceremony with every outsider and every newborn to check their soul."

We rested in quiet for one minute or two until she broke

the silence.

"Can I ask you a question?"

"Of course, go ahead," I said.

"Why did you invite me to Izah?"

This question baffled me. Why did I invite her to Izah? I dug deep in my heart, and I found the answer.

"Well..." I said. "I guess I felt an intense curiosity about you. I wanted to know you, smell you, have sex with you next to the fireplace and have children with you. I liked you from the first moment we met."

She kissed me.

"And why did you come?" I asked.

"For the same reason that you invited me, except for the weird voyeur fireplace sex." She laughed.

"We don't need to do it in front of others if it bothers you."

"Don't worry, I think I'll be okay with that."

Mary Jane established herself in our hut. Spring came, and warm weather brought a good season of fruits and groceries. She explained to me a lot of things about the outsiders. They had televisions where they could see other people recorded from another place in the world. She told me that some men traveled to the moon two years ago, and it was broadcasted live on TV. The more information about the outsiders she shared with me, the more interested I got. I started doubting our traditions and way of life, considering that there was such a huge amount of people living in a totally different, unknown world.

One year after Mary Jane settled in Izah, we had our first child, Jonas. Mary Jane held him on the ceremony stone, watching proudly as all the villagers climbed one by one on the stone to observe and smell the newborn. I recalled when Mary Jane stood there for the first time and how she had looked at that very moment. Now she seemed confident and proud of who she had become, and it was me who was scared and trembling about the future awaiting Jonas.

FATE

David was punctual as always. He planned to arrive at least thirty minutes before the job interview, in case something would happen on the way like a delay with the train or a terrorist attack that would collapse the city. He stepped out of Central Train Station and headed to the building where he had the interview. He had memorized the way at home so he didn't need to take the phone from his pocket to check Google Maps.

At the corner of the train station, a woman crashed into him. She was a seventy-year-old gypsy, short, with brown skin and blue eyes. She was covered by a dark jacket and a hood. She put herself in front of David and stared at him.

"I'm sorry, madam," said David. "I don't have any cash to give you."

David tried to pass her, but the woman moved in front of him, not letting him pass.

"Excuse me, madam. I am in a hurry. I am really in a hurry."

No answer from the woman, who kept gazing at David, making him feel awkward and stressed. She opened her mouth after a few seconds.

"I can help you understand it," said the gypsy woman.

"Understand what?"

David got tired of waiting and sprinted, leaving the woman behind. He didn't want to be late to the job interview. *I can help you understand it.* Understand what? David couldn't take this sentence out of his head while waiting in the cold corridor of the office where he had the interview. A fluorescent light flickered, which made him feel tense. He had to wait almost one hour until they called him.

The interview was a disaster. "Thank you for coming, David. We will let you know if you get to the next step." David had been already unemployed for two months, and even though he had some savings to live on for more than one year, he was stressed. *They will not hire me, for sure,* he thought.

While coming back to the train station, he thought again about the gypsy woman. *She just wanted to fool me to get some coins.* He passed through the same point where the woman had stood, but she was not there. David ambled around the station and in the park out front. He sat on a bench and waited. There was no trace of the gypsy woman. He wanted to tell her that she didn't trick him, that he knew that she just wanted money. He wanted to tell her that he didn't get the job because of her. He wanted to tell her that he was angry.

At his small apartment in the suburbs, David prepared a sandwich and tea and sat in the kitchen. *What does it mean, I can help you understand it? What do I need to understand?* Far from getting calmer, the tea made him more jittery, so he broke his daily routine and went out for a walk. It began to rain, softly, and the drops felt heavy on his face like the pressure of finding a new job. But he couldn't stop wondering about the gypsy woman.

David started the next day as usual. Coffee and toast on the sofa with the laptop on one side to look for job offers. Nothing interesting. His legs trembled, and he couldn't find a comfortable position on the sofa, so he went for a walk again. His subconscious took him to the train station. He tried to empty his mind, thinking about random stuff like how birds were able to fly, how controllers managed to handle all the trains that arrived almost at the same time in the stations and used the same rails... Without noticing it, he got off the train in Central Train Station. *What am I doing here?* He rambled around, and in the corner where the day before he met the gypsy woman, he stopped. *What do I need to understand? With what can you help me?* The gypsy woman was not there. She wasn't in the park either. David strolled through the narrow streets from the center without being able to find her. In the evening, he was exhausted and came back home. That night, he could barely sleep, thinking about her face.

He gave her a name: Fate. He didn't know exactly what he meant by naming her like this, but he found it appropriate. Every morning, he took the train to Central Train Station and marched around the center. Sometimes, he saw a woman with a dark jacket and a hood, and he sprinted to her to ask what she could help him understand. But it was never Fate.

After three weeks of unsuccessful searching, he had completely forgotten about his job. He was obsessed with what he had to understand. He left his apartment in the suburbs and rented a small studio in the center, so he didn't need to lose time by taking the train to Central station.

He began to get familiar with the beggars and the usual drinkers that sat next to the door of the station. One day, one of them caught his attention.

"What are you looking for?" he asked.

"It's none of your business," David answered.

"It's not my business, but I am here lying and drinking every day from morning to evening. I know everything that is going on in here." The beggar laughed, exhaling a putrid breath and showing his five remaining yellow and rotten teeth.

"Okay," said David. "I am looking for a woman."

"What a coincidence! I am too." The beggar found himself so funny that he spilled some of his drink on the floor.

"I am looking for a gypsy woman. She is about seventy years old, brown skin, blue eyes. When I saw her, she wore a dark jacket with a hood."

"Gypsy, eh? There are no gypsies in this area. We don't get along well together. You'd better look in Maire."

"In Maire? The neighborhood? I've never been there."

"Yes, Maire. But be careful with the gypsies. You don't wanna have problems with the gypsies." The beggar took a sip of his drink.

"Okay, thank you."

David gave him some coins for the information. It was already late, and he went back to his small studio. Maire was a neighborhood in the outskirts of the city. David just knew about it because of what he had heard on the news on TV. Apparently, it was a dangerous area, one of the places with higher crime rates in the country. He wondered again if his obsession had any logic, but at this point, he felt that he had already gone too far to leave it. He believed he was very close to finding her. The next day, he would take the train to Maire to find Fate.

The night was long. David stood on a sandy beach next to the river mouth. It was windy and a chilly breeze touched his back, but the cold sand was pleasant to his bare feet. A tiny boat crossed the river in the direction of the sea, a small, dark figure on it rowing with a long stick and finally disappearing into the horizon.

The next morning, he went to Maire by train. The station was small, and the first impression was that it was kind of new. But some of the automatic doors were broken, the floor was sticky, and there was graffiti everywhere. The exterior of the station didn't look better.

David realized he didn't have a plan. He decided to start by walking around the station. He wanted to have the safety of a quick escape in case the events turned bad. The place was awful. There was rubbish on the floor next to the garbage can that was also full, which left a nasty smell. It was obvious that the city didn't care about that area. David didn't see any police cars or taxis. The few people that he met stuck their eyes on him, making him feel like a total stranger. He spent just one hour there and returned to his studio, without any clue on how to find Fate.

He repeated the same process every day, exploring a little more of Maire to get used to the area, like a dog that was brought to a new house. But he knew that just by rambling around, he would not get to Fate. He would need to ask.

He met a group of three men sitting on a window sill, drinking and chatting. David considered that they looked pretty inoffensive.

"Excuse me, sirs," said David. "Can I ask you a question?"

They gazed at him, then they looked at each other and laughed.

"Sirs? Ha ha ha! It's the first time someone has called me sir since my son-in-law asked for my daughter's hand. My name is Abraham."

"Nice to meet you, Abraham. I'm David."

"My name is Paddy," said the man sitting next to Abraham, "and this drunk one is Duke. Come sit and drink with us!"

"Thank you, but I am not really a drinker..." said David.

"Come on, Gorger!" said Abraham. "Do you wanna ask us a question? We will have some fun together, and then you can ask your question."

"All right, then."

David took a sip directly from the bottle that they were drinking. His face turned red, and he felt a fireball going down his throat. The three men laughed at David's face.

"What is this? It's strong!" said David.

"It's vodka with lemon juice. We like it," said Duke.

"So, David, isn't a Gorger like you afraid to come to Maire?" asked Abraham. "People from the city don't come here. They think we're criminals. It's what they say of us on TV."

"I was afraid in the beginning...from what I heard about this place." David felt he said too much, but the three men listened to him thoughtfully. "But now I see that I didn't have any reason to worry."

"This is because of the vodka!" Paddy laughed.

They chatted for more than an hour until they finished the bottle. David learned about their traditions and lifestyle. It had been a very long time since he talked for as long with someone.

"Now, tell us, Gorger. What was your question?"

"I am looking for a woman. I want to know if you can help me find her."

"We are all family here," said Abraham. "We know each other. If she lives in Maire, we'll know her. What's her name?"

"I don't know her name. I don't know much about her. I just met her once in Central Train Station. She is a woman of about seventy years old, brown skin, blue eyes. She wore a dark jacket with a hood."

The three gypsies got serious and stared at each other. David caught their reaction.

"Do you know her?" asked David.

"She doesn't live here," said Abraham.

"But yes, we know her," said Paddy.

"Where can I find her?"

"You can't. She finds you." Abraham looked sober for the first time in the whole conversation. "But you don't want to find her. She is death. Did she touch you?"

"No, she didn't... She told me, 'I can help you understand it.' And I don't know what she meant."

"You will need to figure it out by yourself, then," said Paddy. "She won't come back to you, hopefully."

What they said discouraged David. He would not understand it by himself. He didn't even know what it was about. They said goodbye, and David promised to visit them soon to chat and drink vodka.

On the way back by train, he wondered about death. He thought about his father, who died when he was seven. Some flashbacks from his death came to him: the hospital, his mother crying, the funeral. He didn't understand what had happened and nobody explained it to him. He became a solitary child, and when he got older, he sheltered himself in routines to hide his insecurities.

He felt released after this thought, like he had exchanged a couple of metallic boots that attached his feet to the ground for comfortable, light, and soft slippers. He felt grateful to Fate. He would come back to the gypsies one day next week, with the confidence of someone who understood himself a little more.

WINTER

Brother Jamie was the fourth one in two weeks. His funeral was a sober ceremony, a simple farewell conducted by Prior Phillip where all the monks could say goodbye to Jamie. The intense winter crashed heavily on the stone walls of the monastery and squeezed everything to death.

I was the one who found the dead body of Brother Jamie. It had been early morning when I left my room because of my recent dizziness and tottered to the latrines. Brother Jamie lay on the floor, facing down, cold as a frozen lake, with his skin covered in livid bruises. The nauseating smell mixed with the latrine waters and the early putrefaction stage of Jamie's body made me puke, leaving an even more disgusting scene. I summoned other brothers for help, and between four of us, we took Jamie's body to a more decent location. I noticed he had some scars on his arms and legs, as if he had been hiking in a dense bush forest or had an encounter with an angry cat.

I had assumed that the previous death of our three brothers were accidental, an inevitable fate from the violent, freezing winter. We found their bodies in their rooms within three days of each other after noticing that they didn't attend the morning prayer. But the recent demise of Brother Jamie made me wonder and consider other possibilities. How could he walk to the latrines and die from coldness in there? What were the scars he had on the arms and legs?

I decided to bring up the topic during the daily convention the afternoon after his funeral.

"Dear brothers. There is no doubt that winter is striking in our community. The calamitous loss of four of our brothers left us speechless." Everybody nodded at my words. "But there are some strange things in the departure of our brothers."

"What do you mean by this, Brother Anthony?" asked Prior Phillip.

"During the whole of last winter, we had just one funeral, Prior. And two winters ago, we buried only one brother as well. I was just considering the possibility of a non-natural death." I noticed the eyes of the prior glaring daggers at me.

"And how could the death have happened, if not in a natural way?" asked Prior.

"Brother Jamie had scars on his arms and legs. Maybe something or someone caused his death." A long murmur went across the room.

"This is unacceptable! Nobody from outside can enter our monastery. And I will not accept any insinuation of murder from one of our brothers. We are all sons of God, and the loss of our brothers is God's will. Today's convention is over."

I was not surprised by the reaction of Prior Phillip. He was very conservative, and he would avoid any kind of changes and confrontation. I had the hunch that something external caused the death of our brothers, and it would keep happening if someone didn't stop it. I decided to investigate.

I visited Brother Jamie's room that night. It was similar to mine. A simple, tiny stone room with one bed and a desk. The bed was still unmade, and everything was in its place. There was no sign of violence of any kind. Half of a candle stood on the desk next to an open Bible. He was reading Job 1:7. "The Lord said to Satan, 'Where have you come from?' Satan answered to the Lord, 'From roaming throughout the earth, going back and forth on it.'" I was about to leave the room when something caught my attention. On the floor, there was a small wooden ball that looked like one of our rosary beads. I looked under the bed, and I couldn't spot the rest of the rosary. Maybe it was Jamie's rosary that broke days ago, or maybe it was someone else's, damaged during a brawl with Brother Jamie. I would try to find out the next morning during the first prayer.

That night, I could barely sleep. The image of Brother Jamie lying inert on the latrine's floor passed continuously through my mind, and I couldn't stop speculating on the possibility that one of us was responsible for it. What was the purpose? Was there any link between the four deaths? I started to get a headache and finally, I fell asleep with plenty of unanswered questions.

The next morning, we followed the daily routine. The bells rang to wake us up. Everybody ambled to the chapel in absolute silence. There was a restrained tension between the brothers after our last convention, and the frigidness of the dawn and the dimness of the chapel made the oratory a very unpleasant place to remain. Everybody focused on their own prayers, counting their rosaries. I pretended I was praying as well, but I had an open eye to examine the others in the gloom. I sat on the second bench, and from where I stayed, I couldn't spot anybody without a rosary. I glanced up at the altar for an instant. The prior was not praying. He was sitting on his chair, just observing us. I realized I had never noticed if he was praying like the rest of us during our morning ritual or not, but that day, he was definitely not doing so.

I spent the next few days observing the monastery and each of our routines. I had always been so focused on praying and studying in my room that I had never stopped for a moment to admire our building and surroundings. Life in the monastery was quiet and monotonous. Some brothers spent the mornings treading around the cloister, others rambled through the garden. The library was always full of souls aiming for increasing their knowledge and wisdom.

I was sitting in the cloister witnessing the winter twilight when Prior Phillip came to me.

"Brother Anthony, would you join me for a moment in my chamber?"

"Yes, of course, Prior."

We walked in silence to his room. It was much bigger than ours, replete with golden chandeliers of long red candles. He had a few open books on his desk, and a small brazier warmed up the room.

"I know you checked Brother Jamie's room a few nights ago." He startled me. I was almost sure nobody had seen me.

"I just wanted to say goodbye to him. Jamie and I were very close." I felt like Prior Phillip was examining me, and I was sweating.

"I made it clear that the recent loss of our brothers was a result of the freezing winter. God wanted to take them with Him, and we can't contradict God's will. I forbid you to do any further investigation on their deaths. Otherwise, you will be expelled from our community."

"Yes, Prior. My apologies."

"You can leave now."

I went back to my room. I was disappointed and confused. The wind blew strong from outside, and a cool breeze seeped through the walls. I fell asleep wishing I owned a brazier in my room like Prior Phillip.

A loud scream woke me up, before the bells rang for the first prayer. I jumped out the bed and staggered outside. Again, I had that annoying dizziness that affected me recently, like everything moved in circles around me and the walls were about to fall on my head. I tottered to Brother Filbert's room. Brother Vincent remained next to the door with a pale face.

Brother Filbert lay on the floor with a small thread of dry blood coming from his nose. He was dead.

"What happened?" I asked Brother Vincent while other brothers showed up, awakened by his scream.

"I heard some weird noises and couldn't sleep. When they stopped, I went to the latrines, and I saw that Brother Filbert's door was open. I went inside, and I found his body."

I checked Filbert's body. He had some scars on his neck and arms, similar to the scars on Brother Jamie. On the desk, there was a Bible opened to Matthew 13:25. "But while everyone was sleeping, his enemy came and sowed weeds among the wheat, and went away. The weeds are the people of the evil one, and the enemy who sows them is the devil."

Prior Phillip arrived when the sound of the bells rang, indicating the arrival of a new winter morning. "Everybody, out of here! Brothers, it is time for praying. Move to the chapel!"

We all went down to the chapel in silence, even Prior Phillip. We left the body of Brother Filbert in his room, lying alone. I glanced at Brother Vincent's face, still pale, tears on his cheeks. Everybody was scared, but the praying remained silent as always.

That afternoon, we buried Brother Filbert. He was the oldest one in our community. A wise monk, always willing to smile and help you enhance your knowledge. The rain wet our robes while we dug the hole in the cemetery, falling in a tense stillness. It was a cruel winter.

That night, I decided to seek for answers in the Bible. Brother Jamie and Brother Filbert had opened chapters on their desks that both mentioned the devil. I had always been frightened of the devil, and I used to skip those parts of the Bible that talked about it with the idea that my ignorance about Satan would make it disappear.

The heavy rain made the humidity sneak into my bones,

and my hands shook because of the crisp air. I noticed I had a lot of notes in my Bible that I wasn't aware of. John 3:8 said, "The one who does what is sinful is of the devil, because the devil has been sinning from the beginning. The reason the Son of God appeared was to destroy the devil's work." Peter 5:8 said, "Be alert and of sober mind. Your enemy the devil prowls around like a roaring lion looking for someone to devour." I got dizzy, my mind felt trapped in a cage that floated on the sea water during a thunderstorm. My jaw was tense and my teeth ground together, and a sudden heat rang through my body.

I stared at my hands. My fingers had long black claws. I was not cold anymore and a foam of stinky vapor emanated from my body. I ran out of my room and dashed to the prior's chamber. He opened his eyes, and I could see my reflection in his pupils. I observed his distressed face as I choked him to death.

I was the devil.

LONE

One more day on Earth. Mike awakes with the first sunlight coming in through the huge windows of the suite where he slept last night. He stands, opens the windows, and emits a loud screech. Nothing, just the echo of his own scream and the sound of some birds flying away. The rest, silence.

He walks down the stairs. Eleven floors. *Next time, I will choose a one-story house*, he thinks. He passes through the hallway and rings the bell from the reception desk several times. "The bill!" he shouts. He walks away, giggling. "This is always funny," he says to himself.

He ambles next to lots of luxury cars parked on the street, as the hotel where he slept is located in a posh area. *It is such a sunny day today. I'm gonna take a convertible.* He finds a beautiful black Porsche 911 Targa from 1981, gets in the car and manages to turn on the engine by hotwiring it. "Voilà!" The sound of the engine is deep and potent. The FM radio, of course, just emits a snowy noise, but Mike has brought some cassettes and CDs. He chooses 'Stuck in the Middle with You' from Stealers Wheel. He puts on his sunglasses and starts driving without aim. "I love this life."

The event occurred exactly three months ago, on March 21. Mike was still forty-nine years old when he woke up in his small apartment that morning, unwilling to go to work as always, grumping and complaining. He left the apartment and headed to the metro station, got inside and waited on the platform. Three minutes, five minutes, fifteen minutes. He looked around, and he noticed for the first time that day that he was alone. He came back to the street and there was nobody. No taxis, no buses, no people stomping to work, no open kiosks, no open cafes. *This is very weird*, he thought. He strode to work and arrived after forty-five minutes. Nobody there either. He waited one hour and went back to his apartment. He turned on the TV to see that the screen was just showing white noise. Later on, that night, the electricity cut off, while the tap water still flowed. He realized the next morning that every single human had vanished from Earth between night and day without leaving any trace. Every human being, except for him.

Burning up the road with his Porsche through the beach promenade and listening to the Beach Boys, Mike wonders what he is going to do today. He stops at a stationery shop and grabs some markers and sprays, and he drives to the National Art Museum. He always carries a crowbar in order to break into places. Once inside the museum, he vandalizes the most famous and classical paintings with fake mustaches, guns, funny eyes, and dicks. "This is hilarious!" he screams. When he gets bored, he drives back to the beach promenade to grab ice cream.

While sitting in the middle of the road and enjoying his stracciatella with white chocolate, a loud blast disturbs him. It sounds like an explosion. He focuses in the direction from where he heard the noise. Another detonation is followed by a small cloud of smoke that stands in the air. *Fireworks?* His face changes completely. *Fuck, there is someone else besides me!* He hustles to turn on the car again and speeds to the opposite side of the city. He can hear the fireworks bursting behind him.

He arrives at a five-star hotel with an open revolving door. *Today, I am staying on the second floor.* He opens the minibar, takes a bottle of Jameson whiskey and pours it into a glass. He stands next to the window. *Who else is in this city?*

he thinks. *I don't want any neighbors. This is so perfect. I can do what I please and nobody disturbs me. Maybe I've been too loud those days?* Through the window, he can recognize the smoke left from the blasts of the fireworks in the distance. As it is still sunny and warm, he takes the bottle of Jameson and climbs the stairs to the rooftop swimming pool.

That night, he can barely sleep. Every fifteen or thirty minutes, there is a detonation from a firework. He has a nightmare about his life before the event, when he was forced to meet other people at work, in the stores and on public transport, and the pressure to have contact with others as a part of an unwritten social contract.

The next day, Mike wakes up a little later than usual. The sun is already high up, and he is more hungover than any day before. *That Jameson was for sure refilled!* He stumbles out of the hotel debating whether to take a Tesla or a Harley Davidson, still carrying the Jameson bottle in his hand.

He stops and drops the bottle on the floor. An elderly woman and a teenage boy are standing in front of the hotel staring at him. *No, no, no! I can't fucking believe!*

"I am so glad to meet you!" says the old woman, smiling. "My name is Betty, and this is Mathew," she says, pointing at the boy.

"Hi..." Mike answers. "How...how did you find me?"

"We moved to the city after hearing the message on the radio a few days ago. We followed the fireworks, and later in the night, we heard someone singing from the top of the hotel. I guess it was you."

Mike frowns. *I drank too much whiskey last night.*

"A radio message?" asks Mike.

"Yes, there's more of us! They're shooting fireworks to guide us. They're on the other side of the city, just a few kilometers from here. Let's walk there together."

"Eh...well... No, thank you. I'd rather be alone."

"Alone?" says Betty. "We're all alone! We can help each other!"

"I'm glad that you can get help from others, but me... I. Would. Rather. Be. Alone!"

Mike gets in the Porsche 911 and flees from there, leaving Betty and Mathew staring at him. *Those annoying people! I couldn't even find a Tesla!*

He feels hungry, so he goes to the supermarket to grab some canned food. The fireworks are still audible from time to time. In the store, he opens some crisps after checking that they are not expired and takes some tuna cans for later. He also picks a Four Roses American Whiskey. All of a sudden, he hears someone yelling. *Oh, please! Can this day get any worse?*

"Help! Help!"

The yelps come from inside the supermarket. Mike follows the sound that leads him to a big door next to the meat shelves. He knocks on the door.

"Everything all right in here?" Mike asks.

"Help! Please, open the door!"

"Why are you in there?"

"Open the fucking door! I'm freezing!"

Mike opens the door using a handle. Inside the small chamber, there's a guy, about thirty years old, shaking, who sprints out the door and stands next to Mike.

"Give me this!" says the guy while taking the bottle of whiskey from Mike's hand. He opens it and takes a big sip.

"That's mine!" says Mike.

"I'm Ken. Thank you for opening the door and saving my life. And for the whiskey," he says, raising the bottle.

"My name is Mike. Why did you get in the freezer?"

"Survival tip. There's still fresh meat inside them; the coldness stays even without electricity."

"Good to know."

"Are you also going to meet the others?" asks Ken.

"No, no, no, no... No, I'm...on my own. I'm enjoying my isolation."

"Ah, I understand, a lone wolf. I don't really trust the radio message, but I want to see what's going on in there. I have nothing to lose. By the way, do you know how to hotwire a car? I'm tired of going by bike."

"Yes, of course, I'll show you how to do it."

Ken chooses a white Volkswagen Multivan parked in front of the supermarket. Mike teaches him how to turn it on without a key.

"Thank you, Mike. I hope to see you soon."

"Good luck, Ken."

Mike observes how Ken departs, finding himself alone holding a bottle of whiskey in one hand and a bag of crisps in the other. *Finally alone!* he thinks. *It's time to relax.*

He drives away in his Porsche, combining every change of gear with a sip of whiskey. He now selects a more somber mood for driving with 'The Night We Met' by Lord Huron. While at the wheel, he focuses on the fireworks that are still exploding in the distance and wonders how many people are already together and what they might be doing right now. *Are they partying? Or are they planning how they're going to organize the next survival society? Maybe one day I could visit them. Ken looks like a good guy; it actually felt good to talk with him. After all, we are all survivors of an unknown event that changed the world.* While bringing the bottle of whiskey to his mouth, the front left wheel of the car bumps into a hole on the asphalt, leading Mike to try to turn the car rapidly, followed by a sequence of violent flips that ends in a brutal crash into a wall, leaving the car upside down.

Mike is trapped in the car, half unconscious. *There is no ambulance that will save me,* he thinks. He struggles to escape from the car, unsuccessfully. He is about to faint when he spots a white van moving toward him. It's Ken. He manages to drag Mike out of the car and helps him to lie on the floor.

"Man, you need to drive more carefully! You completely destroyed your Porsche!"

Mike stands, teetering, and tries to articulate his words.

"Thank...you," says Mike. "You saved my life."

"No problem, Mike. You saved mine. Good luck on your journey."

Ken walks to his van and gets inside.

"Wait!" shouts Mike. "I'm coming with you."

Ken gazes at Mike from the van with a smile.

"I didn't have any doubt you would, lone wolf."

THE FABRIC OVER THE MOON

LOCKED

Sometimes I think I would like to be a builder, spending hours outdoors constructing the tunnels and connections from buildings. Or a transporter. Or something that would allow me to be outside a few hours per day.

Instead, I studied Chemistry. "It's going to be the degree with more jobs!" they said. Yes, I have a job, a good position. And it's extremely boring.

Every day, I wake up at 7 a.m., I eat some soy mousse, and I take the tunnels to the plant. I can go on foot; it takes me about twenty minutes to get there. On the way, through the cold dark gray walls, I peer at the monotonous faces of the pedestrians, some listening to music, others looking at the advertisements on the screens of the tunnels, others taking the automatic line and standing with faces on their phones... I like to walk, just walk and nothing else.

In the plant, I am in charge of checking that there is a correct balance in the transformation from nitrogen oxide and carbon dioxide into oxygen. It is pretty monotone. I have a lunch break where I meet Adam and Josh, two of my friends from university that also work in the plant. We usually eat a soy protein bar and some grain pudding. Then, I go back to work for four more hours.

If I don't go to the gym after work, I usually walk through the garden. There are five trees and some plants. I find myself relaxed next to the trees. They are impressive, very big, and they have some leaves that sometimes fall on the ground. When

I find one leaf, I always take it home with me; it means that it was a good day. They say they will build more gardens in the future. They actually tried to make another one close to where I live, but unfortunately the plants couldn't grow there. We have been told that there are other cities that have far more of them. I would really like to visit them.

I can't imagine how life was before. They explained it to us at school in history class, in biology class, and in chemistry class. To me, it looks like something impossible to be true, like a fairytale or a book talking about a magic boy. When teachers talked about it, their eyes got wet and smaller. Sometimes they stared at infinity with a brief smile, and sometimes they looked directly to the floor and wiped a tear from their faces. When I was born, apparently it was still possible to go out. My parents explained to me that they used to take me outside every day when I was a baby, just for a few minutes, before you started to feel a lack of breath. "To see the world," they said. Of course, I don't remember anything about that.

The atmosphere changed very quickly. In three years, governments and cities had to rush to build oxygen plants and cover the streets. I know that some countries did it quicker and in a better way, with a lot of tunnels made by transparent glass so you can see the sky and a lot of connections between the cities. In my country, we are going slower. My city is still isolated, and we don't know when we'll have the first connection built. They say it might arrive in ten years. But at least we have tunnels and oxygen plants. They estimate that ninety-three percent of the world population died in the last twenty years because they were not able to prepare the cities, so I feel grateful for being where I am.

When I have the opportunity, I always go outdoors. At work, they allow us to go outside for one hour every week. It's the most exciting thing I do in my life. My colleagues Adam and Josh don't want to come, they say there's nothing to see out there. I always find something new outside. They give us masks and oxygen tanks, and we walk around the plant. The idea is to check if everything from outside works fine, if there is a fissure on the walls or if the smoke is not going out as it should. Once, I found a beetle. I didn't know what it was, and I couldn't catch it. But I asked my biology teacher, and she explained to me that it was probably a beetle. It was beautiful, about five centimeters long, dark brown and with a lot of long and thin legs that moved at a high speed. I didn't know that beetles could live outside, I thought that all the animals had to live indoors, the same way as humans. I would love to have animals in my city.

Sometimes I dream about the past world. I don't know exactly how to imagine it. I have just seen some pictures from school, and some videos that are not banned. Cities without tunnels where you can see the sky every time you tilt your head up, with the sun, the stars, and the moon... A place where you can walk outside without any mask and oxygen tank. I dream about forests, with dozens of trees one next to another, and plenty of animals living there. And the sea, a huge infinite blue hole full of water where you can't see its end. And I wish I would wake up and be there.

FRIEND

"All right, Charles. I am Dr. Ackerman. Do you know why you're here?"

Dr. Ackerman was a tall man, one of those people that looked gigantic, with big hands that could crash a metal streetlight and a square-shaped face. He sat behind an old, dark wooden desk, and his room was filled with books. There was a metallic sign on the desk with his name written on it: 'Dr. Ackerman, Psychiatrist.'

"Not really," I said, "but I guess it's something related to my accident."

"Your parents wanted you to see me after you almost drowned in the sea. It is dangerous to swim in such a storm, even for a seventeen-year-old sporty guy."

He waited a few seconds for my reaction. I didn't say a word.

"When emergency services rescued you from the water and you were unconscious, you were asking for Ted. Ted. Does this name mean something to you?"

I couldn't remember exactly the first time I saw Ted. I wondered it a lot of times. He was in all my memories, always standing a few meters from me and staring at me, without saying a single word or showing any emotion on his face.

Ted was a teddy bear. I named him when I was a child. My parents got worried when I first talked about Ted to them. But I didn't see anything wrong with him; he was not scary for me. As I kept on seeing him, they arranged some sessions with the school psychologist. She told me that Ted didn't exist, that he was in my imagination, that it was okay to have an imaginary friend, but I needed to know that Ted was not real. She was not very convincing for me. She was young and looked inexperienced, and she seemed to be scared of dealing with a child who was seeing a teddy bear that no one else could see.

I decided to pretend that Ted disappeared. For my parents, but mostly to not be forced to go to any more sessions with the psychologist and have those awkward silent moments when she didn't know what to say and we stared at each other like idiots.

But Ted remained with me. Always a few meters apart, peering at me, without giving any sign of communication. I learned to keep him a secret. I tried to not look at him too often when I was around other people to not make it visible that I could still see him.

"Charles," said Dr. Ackerman, who waited for my response for too long, "is this name, Ted, familiar to you?"

I knew I couldn't lie, so I wanted to answer his question to get out as quickly as possible.

"Yes. My parents probably told you already. Ted is a teddy bear, who apparently only I can see."

"Is Ted here with us now?" he asked.

I looked around, but I already knew the answer. He never came in small spaces; he needed more distance. Maybe he was outside the door.

"No. This room is too small for him."

"How long have you known Ted?"

"I don't remember the first time. Ever since I can remember, he has been with me. So I know him from always, I guess."

"Does he talk to you?"

"No. He just stands and looks at me. Look, I already talked with the school psychologist about Ted. I don't think I can get something profitable from this meeting."

"Whenever you want to stop, just tell me and we will stop. So about Ted... Is he good, or is he bad?"

So many questions was starting to bother me, but this one made me think. Was he good or bad? I never considered it before. He was always with me, but his actions looked neutral. Anyway, I jumped to the sea to save him when he was drowning, and I had to be rescued, so I guessed I considered him as a good being.

"For me, he is good. It's not that he does something special for being good, he is just with me all the time."

"But you jumped in the water because of him, right?" Dr. Ackerman asked.

"He was drowning, I just wanted to save him!"

"And you almost died. Tell me, Charles... One week ago, you were almost hit by a bus when you crossed the road without looking. Were you also trying to save Ted?"

I was stunned. Nobody knew about it, or that was what I thought. A few days ago, I was coming back from school when I saw Ted in the middle of the road. A car was about to crash into him, so I ran towards him to save him. All I heard was a loud horn that left me paralyzed. A bus that came from the other side had to brake suddenly and stopped a few centimeters from me. I felt my heart was about to escape from my mouth. Everything happened so quick. I put myself together and looked ahead. Ted had been standing in the same spot, impassive as always, staring at me.

"Yes," I said. "Ted was on the other side of the road about to get run over by a car, so I ran to him to save him."

"And again, you almost died. Has he put you in danger before?"

"He doesn't put me in danger."

Dr. Ackerman started to sound insolent to me. Why was he judging Ted if he didn't know him? I didn't know Ted that much neither, but I knew he didn't want anything bad for me. I felt it. Dr. Ackerman noticed that I was uncomfortable with the direction the interview was headed, so he didn't push me more.

"Is Ted real, Charles?"

"Dr. Ackerman, I know the theory: Ted is imaginary, he is just in my head, it's just me who can see him, blah, blah, blah... But tell me, Doctor. What does it mean, real? What is reality? When you have a feeling for a person, nobody can see it, right? But does this mean that it's not real? Millions of people believe in gods that they will never see, they believe in them even without having the smallest sign of their existence. We don't tell them that they believe in something imaginary. Me, I see Ted. This is my proof of his existence."

"You are very intelligent for someone only seventeen, Charles. And why do you think that Ted appears just to you?"

If only I knew... I heard all the conversations from behind the door. I couldn't enter small area, I needed more space to breathe. I had always been with Charles from his childhood. I didn't remember the first time I met him either, nor what I did before. I slept when he slept, I ran when he ran.

What fate it was that linked me to him and made me stay close to him all this time, was a mystery to me. Charles at least knew he was a human. What was I? I knew everything about Charles, but I knew nothing about me.

I tried to communicate with him plenty of times. Always unsuccessfully. I couldn't talk. I couldn't touch him, or even get close to him. The only thing I could do was observe.

I considered the possibility that I didn't exist, that I was just a product of Charles's imagination, like an extension of his mind. Who knew?

Charles was good. He was everything I had. And I also wanted good for him. That was why I tried to kill myself in two occasions recently. First, I stood on the road in front of a car. In my second attempt, I jumped into the sea from a cliff. I wanted to disappear to make his life easier.

I didn't want to cause any more trouble for him. But Charles always followed me, in the same way I followed him.

I guessed that we both realized it during our last incident. There was something that merged us together, an invisible force stronger than us that was uncontrollable. We needed to accept that we would always be together.

I thought for a few seconds before answering Dr. Ackerman's last question.

"I guess that Ted and I just follow each other. There is something that merges us together, an invisible force stronger than us that is uncontrollable. We need to accept that we will always be together."

PARADE

The music was hypnotizing. I didn't know if it was because of my inebriation or because of all those colorful movements that made the whole street look like a luminous chromatic river. I glanced around me and, as I suspected, I was alone. I got lost.

The Carnival in Rio de Janeiro was spectacular. I had never seen so many people moving with such grace and grinning with amusement. I let myself get carried away by the stream of the crowd dancing in the same way a grain was moved during a sandstorm.

I came with Jack and David; it had been our dream trip for ages. We would spend the days of the Carnival in Rio de Janeiro and afterwards we would visit Sao Paolo. To be honest, I was happy to get lost alone, purely enjoying the party in a totally new place by myself.

"De onde você é?" a female voice came from the crowd. A young woman dressed in a green corset with huge colorful feathers and a black eye mask looked at me while dancing and moving two maracas with her hands. She was astonishingly beautiful.

"Excuse me?" I could speak Portuguese, but I hadn't heard her well.

"Where are you from?" She smiled at me. I couldn't hide that I was not Brazilian with my pale skin and ginger hair.

"I'm from Scotland." I had to shout to make myself audible over the music and the noise of the crowd.

"My name is Camila."

She invited me to follow her group with her moves. They

were ten or twelve people, all dressed in green clothes with feathers. I was totally a fish out of water with them, a pale ginger guy with a red mask as the only costume and dancing like a stick, surrounded by fit Brazilian boys and girls with samba flowing through their blood. But I had fun.

We moved forward in the parade, and I became a part of the group. They invited me to some Caipirinhas. Camila danced with me all the time. She explained to me in her not-so-good English that she was originally from a village in the interior of Brazil and moved to Rio two years ago.

I noticed that I was actually the only one drinking Caipirinhas, all the others just drank water or Guarana. I didn't care much, as I was having the most fun of my life.

I didn't know if it was because I was starting to get drunk, but I noticed a weird atmosphere in the group as the parade advanced.

"Levaremos a criança quando passarmos pelo palácio." I overheard the conversation that the two guys next to me were having: "We will take the child when we pass in front of the palace." The sentence was totally taken out of context, but what did it mean? I began to get paranoid. Was I the child they wanted to take? Did they want to kidnap me? I felt like an idiot having those thoughts.

Camila probably saw my face of concern and came closer to me.

"Are you having fun? Or are you too drunk already?"

"I drank too many Caipirinhas, I think."

"Come on, smile and dance! We are still missing the best part of the parade!"

You bet we are, I thought. I had the hunch that they wanted to kidnap me and ask my family for money. They would cut my finger off or an ear and send it to Scotland, but my family didn't have money to pay kidnappers, so they would kill me and throw me in a ditch or I would be used as food for dogs.

I felt trapped, and I didn't know how to escape. I found myself in the middle of a criminal gang, alone in Rio.

I identified a big building in the distance – it looked like a palace. *That is where they want to kidnap me*, I thought. I didn't take more Caipirinhas, but I was still drunk. I struggled to understand what the guys from my group were talking about.

"O filho do prefeito está sozinho com a mãe."

I didn't understand that sentence much, but I figured out that it meant something like, "The son of the mayor is alone with his mother."

So, it was not me who they wanted to kidnap, but the son of the mayor of Rio de Janeiro. Surely, his family was wealthier than mine.

What should I do? I couldn't go to any policemen; they would not believe a drunk Scottish talking in primitive Portuguese trying to convince them that a random carnival gang I just met wanted to kidnap the son of the mayor. But if they would kidnap the son of the mayor, the police would think I was in on it, and if I got caught, I would go to jail, and I didn't want to go to a Brazilian jail. I also didn't want to become a kidnapper and live in the jungle.

As we were approaching the palace, my heart rate rose like the bass of a hard techno song. I needed to do something. I thought about running away and cross fingers that the kidnappers would not go after me. But this would mean a terrible fate for the son of the mayor.

When we were a few meters from the palace, I got an idea. It was such a stupid idea, but it was the only one I had. I placed myself in the middle of the group, and I took off my clothes until I got completely naked, just covered by my red mask.

"What are you doing?" Camila shouted at me.

The crowd that surrounded us shouted and pointed at me,

and soon a group of eight or ten policemen quickly appeared, pushing the rest of the people who were just enjoying the Carnival. They jumped on me and took me with them. Other policemen talked with the rest of the group, probably asking if they knew me. While I was being taken, I gazed at the palace. I thought I saw a woman covering the eyes of her child and taking him inside the building. Nobody knew it, but I was a hero.

HERO

Local hero saves the day. This was the heading of the regional newspaper from the third of November of 1995, with a picture of Peter, a young twenty-two-year-old boy from Stowbridge, completely wet holding a baby. *A brave local boy jumped into Ouse river to save Maryanne's three-month-old child during yesterday's storm.*

Peter didn't know what this situation would bring him. He had strolled back home under the heavy rain after a regular day of work in the restaurant when he overheard a moan coming from the riverbank. Peter loved animals, and assuming that the sound was produced by a duck, he walked to the bushes that grew along the shore. There was not any duck there. Instead, a small baby crawled through the mud. The baby glanced at Peter and smiled. Peter didn't know what to do; he always avoided carrying small children because he had an irrational fear that they could break just by being held or they would simply slip from his arms and crush their head on the ground. But he couldn't leave the baby on the ground next to the river under the heavy rain. Babies were vulnerable beings. He took the child and carried him in his hands. *What do I do now?* He didn't need to speculate much because a large crowd of people showed up after a few seconds.

"He saved the baby! Maryanne, come quick! This guy has Josh!" shouted an old man with joy.

A middle-aged woman with tears on her face dashed to Peter.

"Thank you, God! You, boy, are the savior of my baby! I will always be in debt to you!"

Some policemen and photographers from the press were already taking pictures of the tender scene.

"Yes, I saw him swimming out of the river with the baby," a woman said to a journalist that was taking notes with a small notebook, clearly trying to get some attention.

Peter gave the baby to his mother. The journalists and police encircled Peter.

"What happened? How did you take the baby?"

"Well..." Peter didn't know how to explain himself; he had just been looking for a duck. "I found him in the river."

"Oh! You must be an excellent swimmer to carry the baby with such a strong current as today!" a journalist exclaimed.

"Yes... Thank you. I have to go." Peter got overwhelmed and strode to his home while the crowd was still asking him more details of the story and admired him for his courage. He could hear the group clapping their hands while he moved away.

The next morning, Peter went to work as usual after taking the simplest breakfast at home consisting of a piece of bread with butter and a coffee. On his path to the restaurant, ambling in a slow pace with his eyes on the ground, he noticed other people peeking at him, some children even pointed directly at his face with the subsequent reproach from their mothers.

He was astonished just after crossing the door of the restaurant, when the other waiters were already preparing the tables and stopped what they were doing and clapped their hands.

"Hurray for our hero!"

"Good job, Peter!"

"I knew you were great, man!"

People nodded one by one at Peter and clapped his shoulder. Even Marylin, the prettiest girl in town with whom Peter was secretly in love, focused on Peter and dedicated to him some sweet words.

"Peter! What you did yesterday was so brave! I thought you were a fearful and cold-hearted person, but I see you are courageous and sensitive." She smiled at him and kissed him on the cheek. "We could go on a coffee together after work, if you have time," she said.

"Yes, that sounds great." Peter blushed.

That day, the restaurant was busier than usual. Lots of people from town came on a lunch break, hoping to have the hero as their waiter. He got amazing tips. He could overhear people talking from the tables as he passed with the dishes. "How brave he must be to do it, right?" "I wonder if he already has a fiancée." "He looks so skinny for someone who swam carrying a baby in that current yesterday!"

Far from bothering him, the comments made Peter feel important and start believing in himself. He didn't save any baby, he just picked him up from the shore. But he was used to being treated with indifference by others, and for the first time in his life, everybody considered him as someone meaningful and distinctive.

A journalist visited the restaurant as well and interviewed some of the waiters about Peter's life. Even the local TV showed up to ask some questions.

"How is he?"

"Oh, Peter is kind of an introvert," said a waitress, whose name Peter didn't know because she never said a word to him, "but if you knew him well, you could feel he was hiding something under his mask. What he did yesterday, it didn't surprise me. I knew he was a great person."

Peter noticed that Marylin was getting closer to him that day, using every opportunity to smile at him and touch his arm. In one of their encounters in the kitchen, when they were alone, Marylin whispered to him, "Do you want a blowjob?"

"What?" Peter was astounded.

"Come." Marylin took him to the pantry and pulled his pants down. Peter had never had any kind of contact with a girl before. After one minute, they left the room.

"Thank you, Marylin."

"You're welcome." She smiled. "Before, I asked you to go for a coffee after work, but I forgot I have to take care of my grandmother this evening. We could meet tomorrow."

"It sounds great to me."

It was his best day at work. Even more, it was the best day of his last ten years. On the way back home, Peter couldn't believe how much life had changed for him. He was finally someone, and people noticed him. He pranced through the streets, a big grin on his face. The gray colors of the town looked bright and vivid, and the smooth rain falling on his face was pleasant and refreshing. He forgot that he actually didn't save the baby.

Peter stopped for a moment at the same point where he had found the child. A man about forty years old approached him.

"I saw everything," the man said to Peter.

"What do you mean?"

"I know you didn't save shit. You just found the baby on the shore and picked it up. You liar! You didn't do nothing!"

Peter was first confused and soon distressed. He pushed the guy, and they both fell on the mud and grappled. Peter gripped the guy's neck and choked him.

"You will not ruin my life!" Peter shouted. The man's face turned red and then purple, with the expression of a fish out of water. His face mutated after a few seconds to an inert, scared mask of a dark blue color. Peter took the body and threw it in the river, and he thought about how it drowned while he ran home.

ESCAPE

"Who are you?" asked little Shane. A couple of pink pigs with elegant black suits and ties just snuck into her room while she was sleeping.

"My name is Betty, and he is Molly," said one of the pigs. "We came here looking for help."

"I'm Shane. This is my room, and this is my bed," she said, pointing to where she lay. "How can I help you?"

"We are going to the forest to do a job, but we need someone who carries a candle so we can see the path. Would you come with us?"

"Of course!" said Shane.

She mounted one of the pigs, and they left the room. The pig was comfortable, and Shane was so small that they could carry her without effort.

"Which job are you doing?" asked Shane.

"We are bringing a very important and secret message to the Queen of the Forest."

"And what is this message?"

"We can't tell you," said Molly. "It's a secret!"

They crossed the road from Shane's house, and they fell into the forest. The night was dark and cold, and the leaves of the trees didn't allow them to see the stars. Shane lit a candle. The dim light showed a humid floor, and the hooves of the pigs were getting dirty with the mud.

"You will get your suits dirty," said Shane.

"It doesn't matter, we're pigs." They laughed.

"Do you live in the forest?" asked Shane.

"No, we live on a farm a few kilometers from here. We don't know the forest, so we needed a local to guide us with a light. Then we saw your house, and we thought that it would be a good idea to invite you on our quest."

Shane nodded. She was delighted to have met these new friends. Furthermore, they were carrying her on their back, and she felt like a princess riding a horse.

After thirty minutes of walking, they found a river. The water looked calm and deep, and the other side was far. They needed to cross it, but there wasn't any bridge in their view.

"How will we cross? We can't swim," said Shane.

"Let's follow the river until we find a bridge."

They ambled half an hour more with the water on their side, until they saw a narrow light in the distance, just next to the river. They got closer and discovered a tiny house with a single window.

"Should we get in?" asked Molly.

"I don't know, it can be dangerous," said Betty. "We don't know who lives here. He might be willing to eat us!"

Shane jumped to the ground and ran to the door and knocked.

"Who are you?" A deep voice came from inside the house.

"I'm Shane. I came here with my friends. We want to cross the river."

A big man with a long black beard opened the door. The pigs took a step back, shaking.

"Aren't you afraid of walking in the night in the forest, Shane?" asked the man.

"No, I'm not! Because I am with my friends."

"Come inside," he said.

Shane entered first, followed by the pigs. There was a paltry room with just a bed and big stoves with huge pots of boiling water inside.

"Do you live here?" asked Shane. "It's very small, and you are very big."

"Yes, I live here."

"And what are you doing with all those big pots?"

There was a long silence. Molly gazed at Betty.

"I think he wants to cook us," Betty whispered to Molly.

The tall man stared at the pigs.

"Those pots are not for cooking," he said. He looked back at Shane.

"Do you know rain, Shane?" the tall man asked.

"Yes, I know it! I don't like it when it rains."

"Well, the rain comes from the clouds."

"I know this too!"

"And do you know where clouds come from?"

"Yes, they're made from cotton."

"Incorrect!" The tall man pointed at Shane with his huge finger. "They are made of water. And I am the one making the clouds," he said, showing a smile of pride.

"Wow!" Shane was astonished. "And how do you make them?"

"It's very easy. I take water from the river, and I boil it. I am doing it non-stop. Then, the boiled water becomes clouds, and the clouds rain, and the water from the rain returns to the river."

"Sir," said Shane, "my birthday is on the twenty-fourth of April. Could you not make clouds that day?"

"Okay, Shane, I will not. And now, I will help you cross the river."

They embarked on a small wooden boat. The water almost got inside the boat with the weight of the four individuals.

They said bye to the cloud man and continued marching, with Shane on Molly's back. The suits of the pigs were already completely dirty.

The more they progressed, the denser the vegetation

became. There was not a clear path, and the bushes made them lumber slowly. In the span of a moment, some bushes quivered a few meters ahead of them.

"What is that?" asked Shane.

"Shh! Silence!" said Betty. "It might be a wolf!"

The bushes kept shaking; something was moving towards them.

"I think he saw us! Let's run!" said Molly.

They turned around to run away when they heard a dull voice.

"Heelp! Heelp!"

They looked back and saw a tiny and thin deer.

"What happened to you?" asked Shane.

"I got lost," said the deer. She was sobbing and shivering. "And I am afraid of the dark. I need to find my parents."

"We will help you!" said Shane.

"But Shane... We need to find the Queen of the Forest and deliver to her the important and secret message!" said Molly.

"We will first help the deer, and later we will go to the Queen. We have a lot of time!"

The deer joined the crew. As they didn't know in which direction her family was, they kept marching straight, following their previous path.

"Where do your parents live, deer?" asked Shane.

"We live in a glade, where during the day the sun warms our skin and in the night we can see the stars. But I don't know where it is. Shane, why are you alone? Where are your parents?"

"My parents don't spend a lot of time with me at home; they leave me alone very often. And when they do, they usually argue and fight. Do your parents also fight, deer?"

"No, they don't. My father sometimes fights with other deer, but he always wins because he has the biggest antlers."

"Wow, I want to see them!" said Shane.

The forest became less dense as they forged ahead. They found a wider path to follow.

From the distance, they heard a male voice singing a song. "I take them, I put them in the jar! Then I eat them, they are not far!" A wooden carriage pulled by a donkey approached them. A small fat man with a top hat smoking a pipe and singing was driving the carriage.

"It's the Inquisitor!" said the deer. "Quick, we have to hide!"

They took shelter behind a bush. The carriage passed next to them when Shane sneezed.

"Stooop!" said the man on the carriage, pulling the straps. "Who's there?"

Shane jumped out of the bushes, under the scared glance of her friends.

"Hello, sir! I'm Shane."

"Oh, a little girl... I guess you got lost in the forest. I am the Inquisitor." The small fat man jumped off the carriage. "I have some stuff for sale. Do you want to see it?"

"Yes, please!"

The Inquisitor opened a wooden door from the back of the carriage and took out a box.

"What is in this box, Inquisitor?"

"Look."

He opened the box in front of Shane. It was full of slugs, moving and leaving wet traces.

"Wow, they're beautiful! I want one! Can I have one?"

"Yes, you can. But you have to pay me first."

"Oh, I don't have money."

"That's not a problem," said the Inquisitor. "I don't want money. You can pay...with your soul!"

"I don't want to give you my soul!"

"It's too late..."

The Inquisitor left the box on the floor and raised his

hands to take Shane.

"Leave the girl!" a loud voice shouted from the other side of the path. Two huge antlers rose from the wilderness.

"Dad!" The small deer jumped from the place where she was hiding. The two pigs exposed themselves as well.

"Inquisitor, you will not take this little girl's soul!" said the big deer.

The Inquisitor took a step back and returned to his carriage. He took one slug from the box and ate it, herded the donkey and fled without saying a word.

The big deer gazed at Shane.

"Thank you for taking care of my daughter. Can I help you somehow?"

"We are looking for the Queen of the Forest," said Shane. "Do you know where she lives?"

"Yes, I know. Just follow this path, and when you see the purple rock, turn left until you find the swamp. She lives there."

Shane hugged the small deer, and she and the two pigs pranced to find the Queen. It was still dark night, and the silence prevailed during their jaunt.

"Look!" said Shane. "The purple rock!"

She pointed at a huge shiny stone that had an intense lavender color. Shane had never seen such a pretty rock. In the night, it looked like it kindled its own light. They turned left as the deer indicated. There was no path, and they lumbered through the deep forest.

After walking for fifteen minutes, they reached the swamp. There was a dim light coming from the stars, and a moist vapor emerged from the water.

"We are looking for the Queen of the Forest!" said Molly to the void.

"Who wants to meet me?" a voice gushed from the water. They peered around, but they couldn't spot anybody.

"Queen? Where are you?" asked Shane.

"I am here, right in front of you. Just look down."

There was a small green frog wearing a golden crown a few meters in front of them, standing on a leaf on the water.

"Hello, Queen of the Forest," said Betty. "We have an important and secret message for you."

"I am all ears."

"We come from a farm far away from the forest. A snake came to visit us and delivered an important message for you: 'mosquito season is starting in three weeks.'"

"Thank you so much for this valuable and secret information, pigs. To show you my gratitude, I am giving each one of you one of the lucky stones that this swamp is hiding."

The queen leaped underwater and came back with three small, shiny green stones. She gave one to Shane, Betty, and Molly.

"Wow, it's beautiful! Thank you, Queen!" Shane was so excited about the gift.

"We have to go back now, Queen," said Molly. "We have a long way until we get to the farm."

They went back the same way. Shane yawned.

"I'm sleepy," she said.

"I'm tired as well," said Betty. "We can rest next to this tree for a moment before trekking back."

They lay on the soft grass next to a tree. Shane rested in the middle of both pigs, and their bodies gave her warmth.

"Thank you for being my friends," said Shane with closed eyes, and one second after, she fell asleep.

When Shane woke up, the sun was already high, the morning was warm. The pigs were not there. Instead, three policemen surrounded Shane.

"She's awake!" said one policeman.

"Thank God!"

"Poor girl, she escaped last night from her house," said

another policeman. "How bad you have to feel to leave your home in the middle of the night..."

One of the policemen took Shane in his arms and covered her with a blanket.

"Everything will be good from now on, Shane," he said, looking at her eyes.

Shane smiled and put her hand in her pocket. She admired the shiny green stone that the queen gave her and was reminded of how happy she was during her adventure.

MEMORIES

I am the perfect observer. I am patient, I see time passing, I notice the air moving, I feel what people do.

A few days ago, Jack and Mary visited me. I like Jack and Mary. They have known each other since they were children, and now that they are teenagers, I can feel that their young spirit is taking their friendship to something more. Ah, love! How many couples have I seen falling in love next to me? How many kisses, hugs, passionate sex…? It's beautiful. It makes my life joyful and pretty.

I remember Miller the killer. A good boy, although he was a kid with a disturbed mind. He came here thirteen times before he killed himself. He buried the body of thirteen teenage girls in here. It's a pity that the police never caught him before and gave him the psychological help that he needed. I remember the day that he hung himself. Johnny the farmer was the first one to see his body. He called the police, but the press arrived even before them and took a few pictures of the scene. The police dug up the bodies of the poor girls and quickly connected the suicide with the murders. It was on national newspapers for a few days and vanished from the minds of the people the same way it had appeared. Sometimes I'm amazed at how quick things happen, how fast people forget, how brief the memories of human beings are.

Mr Johnson used to come here very often. It was decades ago. He had a secret that nobody else knew. More or less once a month, he would show up, usually in the deep night, dig a hole in the ground and deposit some gold inside. His avarice made him hide all his gold instead of using it for having a good life. The poor man died young, at the age of thirty-five, from tuberculosis. Nobody knew about his secret gold, which stayed there for three decades until a curious child found it. When the child told his parents about the gold, they couldn't believe it. They went from deep poverty to a life of abundance in one day. They spent all the gold on luxury and stuff that they didn't need, and after one year, they were poor again. How deep do the teeth of human lust and greed bite that they can lose everything they have in the blink of an eye?

This year was extremely dry. It rained no more than ten days in the last nine months. I have grown for centuries. I have been used as a nest for animals, as a shadow for pastors, as a meeting point for lovers, but I start to feel that my branches and my leaves don't grow as strong as they did before. My roots can barely absorb more water from the ground. After decades of existence, my end is close. Trees have the quality of observation and patience to understand human beings even more than themselves. But now that I am dying, my knowledge is going to fall with me; it is going to mix with the ground and rot like my leaves. And my memories will disappear.

HUNT

It was a hard time being a wolf. The scarcity of food that came usually in the winter was even more noticeable because of the amount of hunters. More and more people came to the forest to hunt deer and rabbits. And they also killed wolves, but they didn't kill them for eating. This was something that the wolf couldn't understand. In the past, there was an unwritten compromise between wolves and humans. The wolves would not attack their herds, and the hunters would leave food in the forest for the wolves.

Now the wolf was alone. His pack had died. Some of them because of starvation, some of them directly from the hunter's bullets. Winter was hard, and every day, it was more difficult to find food.

The wolf hadn't eaten a decent meal for more than three weeks and ambled through the forest looking for a perishing animal. He had been eating some mushrooms that grew next to the trees, but they made him sick with nausea.

One day on an early morning, the wolf saw something moving in the bushes. He prepared himself to use the little strength remaining to try to hunt the animal. Wolves usually hunted in groups, this was their method, but alone they were useless. He hid himself behind a tree to jump over the animal when it would pass by. A small girl wearing a red cape and a basket pranced through the deep forest. The wolf jumped in front of her while she was picking some flowers.

"Oh! Hello, wolf!" said the girl. She didn't look scared at

all, which confused the wolf. "My name is Red Hood."

"Hello, Red Hood. I am the wolf. Aren't you scared of me?"

"No, I am not. My dad is a hunter, and if something happened to me, he would come to rescue me."

"What are you doing alone in the forest?" The wolf salivated while smelling fresh meat.

"I'm going to bring some food to my grandmother, who lives in the other side of the forest. She's ill."

The wolf couldn't stand his hunger and jumped on the neck of Red Hood. He bit her soft flesh, and a waterfall of blood, red like her hood, gushed from her carotid artery. She died instantly, no pain, no suffering, no time to realize what was going on. The wolf was good at killing animals without suffering. He killed for survival, not for joy or pleasure. The wolf took the body away from the path and began his feast.

He had not been fed for a very long time. He thought about Red Hood. She told him she was going to visit her grandmother who was ill to bring her some food. The wolf gazed at the basket that Red Hood had with her. There was jam, bread, cheese, and some meat. He tried the meat, but he was disgusted because it was baked. The wolf thought it would be a good deed to bring the food back to Red Hood's grandmother.

He carried the basket with his mouth and bounced to the other side of the forest. On the way, he spotted some hunters searching for food. He hid in the bushes and rested. He wasn't in any rush as his stomach was full. He recalled his pack. His family disappeared directly or indirectly because of humans, either because they hunted their food or because they directly killed the wolves. But he didn't consider having eaten Red Hood as revenge. He would not have killed her if he wasn't hungry. It was purely for survival.

All of a sudden, a hunter shouted.

"Come here! Quickly!"

All the other hunters sprinted there. They were next to the remains of Red Hood's body. The wolf observed the scene from a distance, hidden in the bushes.

"The wolf killed Red Hood!" some of them shouted.

"It was the wolf! It was the wolf!"

"We're going to kill the wolf!"

The hunters marched together through the forest, and more and more hunters joined them on the way. The news that the wolf killed Red Hood spread like a pest. The wolf was scared and worried about his life. He took the basket of food and ran away from the hunters as quick as he could. He couldn't understand humans seeking revenge.

He finally got to a small house in the forest. It was the only house within a few kilometers, and he assumed it was Red Hood's grandma. The door was open, so he entered silently. A nauseating smell filled the air of the small house. An old woman lay on the bed.

"Are you coming to take me?" the old woman asked.

"I just came to bring you some food." The wolf left the basket next to the bed.

"There are a lot of hunters today," said Grandma. "You'd better be careful. They could kill you by accident."

"I will be careful, thank you."

"Have you seen my mother?" the old woman said. "She was sitting just here a few seconds ago."

The wolf was confused by Grandmother's words.

"I didn't see her. She was not here when I came."

"Mmh... Have you seen my mother?"

The wolf felt sorrow for Red Hood's grandmother, and he decided to stay with her. Grandmother ate all the food that was in the basket in ten minutes without saying a word. The wolf noticed that she had been starving. He was reminded of how hungry he had been before, rambling through the forest unable to find any animal to hunt, and eating mushrooms that made him puke... He lay next to the bed and fell asleep.

The yelling of some humans woke him up.

"It has to be here!"

"Let's get inside!"

Four men carrying shotguns came inside the house. The wolf stood quickly and ran. He didn't have anywhere to go, so he tried to jump through the window. He heard a loud explosion, and he felt a huge pain in his leg, like a burning arrow shot through his muscles. He felt on the floor, unable to stand. Then, another bullet pierced his back, and another one in his other leg.

While on the floor, he overheard the hunters before he succumbed to death.

"That terrible wolf wanted to eat this poor old woman. Good that we killed it before!"

Red Hood's grandmother stared at the hunters with the confused eyes of someone who didn't understand what was happening.

"Have you seen my mother?"

OBSESSION

The obsession again. I had every sound in my head, every single note that together would form a majestic harmony, a blast of tones flying like the leaves in the twilight of an autumn day. I stood from the bed and portrayed my thoughts in the pentagram. This melody would hypnotize the Pope himself, make kings renounce their thrones and turn beggars into aristocrats. Nobody would be able to play this composition. Nobody, except for me.

I saw Niccolò Paganini in 1832 during one of his auditions. I witnessed with my eyes what I had heard about him. He truly sold his soul to the devil in exchange for a supernatural ability to play the violin. He seemed possessed while performing, turning his eyes backwards and showing a small white conjunctiva, and moving his long black hair like a furious ocean monster. That evening, I decided to become a genius pianist and composer. The best pianist in the history of humanity.

The time of big orchestras was over. The time of playing for the court was past. The future would consist of great composers playing their own melodies, being the soloists and the protagonists of their own work. And aristocracy? Screw them! Music would be enjoyed by people who really loved it, who appreciated the work and virtuosity of their creators.

In 1837, when I resided in Geneva, I had an encounter with the pretentious pianist Sigismond Thalberg, who publicly claimed to be better than me at playing the piano. What a fool! I proposed to organize a contest with the best pianists of the time: Chopin, Thalberg, Czerny, Hers, and me. Princess Belgroioso and Marie, the Countess of Agoult, were the judges. Needless to say that I was widely victorious. Even more, Marie of Agoult became my lover for eleven years after abandoning her husband. Pity for her, she got too angry at me after our breakup and wrote her novel *Nélida* under the pseudonym of Daniel Stern, which starred a negative and egotistical character based on myself. She ended up in an asylum in Paris.

But even better were the novels written by Olga Janina. Her real name was actually Olga Zielinska. Her books obviously talked about me. She described me as someone banal, hypocritical, highly egocentric and grandiloquent. Quite accurate, if I could say. She unsuccessfully tried to seduce me several times, until one day she came to my house in Pest armed with a revolver and a glass of poison. She wanted to kill me and commit suicide after! I persuaded her to not shoot me by playing her a private concert, but I couldn't convince her to not drink the poison. Fortunately for her, she didn't die. She moved to Paris and wrote one more romantic novel about myself under the pseudonym of Robert Frary: *My friend Franz Liszt*. She was a total lunatic.

I spent the best moments of life composing and playing. During seven years, I traveled through Europe doing a tour, from England to Turkey and from Russia to Portugal. In this period, I probably begot multiple children with my lovers, to whom I enchanted with my romantic melodies. I decided to take out the orchestra from the concerts, and I invented the solo recital. I stopped playing for the aristocrats and the bourgeois in order to take my concerts to big auditoriums where more people could enjoy my excellence on the piano. In a concert where I was playing an 'Adagio' from Beethoven, I was asked to put out a candle on the stage. I ordered the lights be turned off in the room, and I played the composition in perfect darkness, giving the public a magical atmosphere.

And about my obsession... I wanted to compose the best pieces of music ever created. I couldn't sleep at night. I woke up every hour to write down what I had in my head. I stopped drinking alcohol. I stopped eating. I stopped flirting with women. I stopped doing concerts. In 1865, I established myself in the Vatican. The Pope Pius IX visited me almost every week. I wanted to get closer to God in order to stretch my potential. I composed multiple songs, filled with the most demanding techniques. But just when I understood who I was, just when I embraced my past and turned my obsessions into talent, just when I used all my love affairs to help me create harmony, I enhaced my music.

Life of Franz Liszt

CHRISTMAS

The bell rang when the whole family was already sitting at the table, and James, the head of the family, was about to pray to thank the Lord for the Christmas dinner. James's wife, Anne, glanced baffled at him, the same as their grown children, Juliet and William.

"Darling, are we expecting someone?" asked Anne.

"They might be some children singing carols and begging for money," said James.

"I will open the door," said Shana, William's fiancée, while standing from the table. It was the first time Shana met William's family, and she wanted to make a good impression.

There were not any children singing carols behind the door. Instead, a forty-year-old guy got in without saying a word to Shana and moved directly to the living room. He looked like a character from an Indiana Jones movie who hadn't taken a shower for a week because he was on an adventure hunting for hidden treasure.

"Hello, my lovely family!" he said.

"Melvin!" said Anne. She stood and ran to him. "I knew you would come back!"

The rest of the family remained sitting, staring at him with heated eyes, Shana still standing next to the door.

"Who is he?" asked Nora and Grace, Juliet's daughters.

"This is your Uncle Melvin," Juliet answered, showing a grimace of disgust. Both children stood from the table and ambled to their uncle, imitating their grandmother.

"Nora, Grace! Come here," said Juliet, pointing at her daughters' chairs.

There was a brief silence that seemed to last three decades. Everybody looked uncomfortable and awkward, except Melvin.

"What are you doing here?" asked William.

"It's nice to see you too, my little brother." Melvin took Shana's chair and sat at the table.

"This is Shana's place!" said William.

"Shana?" asked Melvin, gazing at Shana, who was already in the living room. "Is she our father's lover? Oh, I am sorry to hear that, Mum, but I knew you would get divorced one day."

"No!" shouted William. "Shana is my future wife."

"Are you getting married?" said Anne. "I'm so happy. Congratulations!"

"Congratulations, Shana," said Melvin. "My brother looks just a little boring, but in reality, he is...very boring." He laughed, shoving William with his elbow. "Come, Shana, take a chair and sit with us."

They all sat around the table, which was prepared for seven people and now was hosting eight, leaving Shana without a plate or cutlery. William was incensed.

"You ruined it! I wanted to announce our wedding to the family during Christmas dinner!" said William.

"It's okay, honey," said Shana. "We shared our engagement with your family, and that's what's important."

"That's right, William, listen to your wife-to-be," said Melvin. "And now, let's eat! I'm hungry."

Anne brought soup and chicken and served the whole family. All eyes were on Melvin.

"Why did you come back after ten years?" asked Juliet. "You left without saying a word. You even missed Andrew's funeral. I'm not going to forgive you for this!" A tear streaked down her cheek as she remembered her husband's death.

"Oh, come on, Juliet!" answered Melvin. "He was such a jerk! You are far better without him!"

Juliet stood from the table and went to the bathroom to wipe her tears away. She came back with her face red and her makeup faded.

"Tell me, son. What have you been doing these ten years? We even thought that you were dead," said Anne.

"Short story, Mum. First, I traveled to Asia, and then to South America. In Bolivia, I joined a drug cartel, and after a few months, I became the leader."

James, who had remained in silence until then, spilled his soup from his mouth.

"You did what?"

"Well, it's easier than it sounds, Dad. In the beginning, we produced and dealt cocaine. Then I proposed to start with crystal meth. Do you know how much cheaper and easier meth is to produce than cocaine? It's insane! This made us grow like foam, and I became the leader."

The whole family was startled by Melvin's story. There was a tense silence that was interrupted by one of Juliet's daughters.

"Mum, what's cocaine?" asked Nora.

"It is a bad word, forget about it!" said Juliet.

"Cocaine, cocaine, cocaine!" Nora and Grace sang a catchy song using the forbidden word.

"Nora, Grace! Go to the kitchen," Juliet shouted. "See what you did?"

"They're children, let them play," said Melvin.

"And what happened after?" asked William. "Why are you here?"

"Well... I had some problems with a rival gang. Basically, they want to kill me. That's why I had to leave the country."

William and Juliet's eyes were flaming. Anne started to hyperventilate and staggered to the kitchen to take a Valium.

"And you dare come here?" said William. "And put all of us in danger? You egotistical asshole!"

"Fucking moron!" Juliet shouted. "I have children! If something happened to them because of you..."

"Well, I see that I am not very welcome in this house anymore... I have something that I brought for you. I will give it to you, and then I will leave."

Melvin dashed out of the house and came back with three black sports bags. He gave one bag to Anne and James, one bag to Juliet, and one bag to William and Shana.

"There is one million dollars in each bag," said Melvin. "They are for you. I am not gonna need it. Do with it what you please. I hope you spend it on something funny."

They looked at each other, and the tension that hung in the room suddenly vanished. Only James didn't look pleased by the action.

"We are not accepting any money from drug trafficking," said James.

"Come on, honey," Anne said to her husband. "With this, we could buy the house on the coast that we always wanted. Let's accept it, please."

"Mmh, okay," answered James, "but Melvin needs to disappear. And we will not tell any of our neighbors about it."

Juliet stood and hugged Melvin. William joined, and both siblings melted into Melvin's arms.

"Thank you, Melvin," said Juliet. "I am sorry for the bad things I said to you."

"Thank you, brother. I will miss you," said William.

Melvin stood and minced to the door, from where he waved at his family and said his last words.

"I wish you the best, family. Don't be worried about me. I will take care!"

He got in his Porsche Cabrio and drove into the horizon.

The whole family came back to their Christmas dinner, now richer than ever.

"In his very core, he is a good person," said Juliet.

"I told you, Juliet," said Anne. "We just needed to give him an opportunity. I hope he will be good."

William couldn't resist and opened the bag. He took a wad of bills from inside, and his face became a puzzle. Instead of Benjamin Franklin, the bills had a picture of Melvin's face, and where it should be written *In God we trust*, there was an infantile drawing of a penis.

"Motherfucker!"

AUTOPSY

"Time of death: around 5 a.m., April 15."

That was four hours ago. This poor girl was attacked in the street, probably when she was coming back from a party, according to the fancy clothes she wore. I can still smell her perfume under my mask.

I cut her Gucci dress with my scissors. Always the same feeling, no matter your past or your background. Once you die, nothing matters.

"She has displayed some lividity in the back of the arms and legs." Justin is writing everything I say. To be honest, I would prefer to do this job alone with a tape recorder than being with him. In the beginning, it was like this, just me and the body and a tape recorder. Far simpler, far more intimate. Now, with the new protocols, there must be two people in every autopsy. Don't misunderstand me. I like Justin, and he is a good helper, but for this kind of job, you want to feel quiet and calm, and take the time that you need for every action.

"There is a five-centimeter incisive injury in the hypogastrium, probably made by a knife. Blunt force trauma in the occipital area, without cranial fracture. There is no signs of rape."

Justin attends to all my movements and explanations without saying a word.

"Scalpel." I open my hand.

I make a large, thin cut through her belly, and I separate her muscles. This action is unnecessary; I already know the cause of death. For the location of the incision and the lividity on her back, the knife must have injured her aorta.

"Cause of death: incision with a knife in the aorta. We are done, Justin. You can go, I will prepare the body for the identification."

"What happened to her?" I don't understand why Justin always wants to know the whole scene. Our work consists of identifying scientifically how a person died, not the reasons and the background. That is left to the police.

"We don't have any identification, and she doesn't have any purse, documents, or phone. So I guess someone just stabbed her to rob her."

"She's young."

"Yes, she was."

"I will help you with the preparation of the body."

"No, Justin, I will do it. Thank you. You can go to the office and close the report."

Justin leaves the room. Finally, I am alone. Having such a young body and only a few hours after death is uncommon. There is a lot of blood that has still not clotted – I can smell it from here.

I have not killed a single person during the last fifteen years. It was a hard decision in the beginning, a far more difficult path for a person like me. I decided it after almost getting caught by the police twenty years ago. They were after me; they thought that I was a serial killer. I was even on the news. Of course, I didn't stop immediately. I couldn't. First, I had to study medicine to become a forensic doctor. During university, I had to be very careful, I couldn't move around with as much ease as I wanted, and finding perfect victims was difficult. But soon, I began to do extra practice in the forensic department, and I could stop killing. Later, I moved to a city with a higher criminal rate, so I would have a lot of autopsies per week.

I always prefer a fresh body, someone who died seconds ago, with warm blood still moving through their veins. But I don't like killing; it is the worst part of it. I can't stand seeing other people suffering, and now I cannot imagine going back to my previous life where I had to hunt.

Let's get started now. Last one I had, it was four days ago. I am hungry, and I have a raw piece in front of me full of blood. I will drink until the last drop.

BLOCKAGE

There was a thin line between inspiration and motivation. Where did one finish and the other started? I sat in front of the screen, fighting against the white page. Five days in a row, eight hours per day. Not a single word.

I used to write like I spoke, as a gossiping widow talking about her neighbors, throwing up word after word with the speed of the wind.

At the beginning, I thought I just had a bad day. Maybe I was ill or something, I didn't know. But the second day, I began to panic. I blamed the spot from where I wrote. The spring sun was getting stronger and penetrated through the window, heating up my back, so I changed my writing place from the living room to the kitchen. It didn't help.

I noticed that my spine hurt after a whole day of sitting in front of the laptop. For sure, this issue thwarted me from performing well in my writing. I spent four hours looking for desk chairs on Amazon. I got it delivered the next day. I had to build it; it took me two long hours. After sitting on it, I felt powerful, like I was resting on a Louis XIV throne. After a whole day in my new chair, my back didn't hurt. But I didn't write a word.

How did the great old writers do it? Dickens, Hemingway, Orwell, Tolkien, Doyle... Surely, they didn't have as comfortable a chair as me. I needed to imitate them.

I drove to the capital to visit a few antiquarians. I spent the whole day moving around stores, talking and debating with unexperienced sellers about typewriters. Finally, I found a beautiful Olivetti Lettera 22 from 1977. A metallic gray, magnificent machine. It was the typewriter used by Leonard Cohen, Paul Auster, Joan Collins, and even Bob Dylan!

I got home, and I couldn't wait to try my new acquisition. I felt like a real writer. I began to type random letters with my Olivetti, and it sounded as if tons of small dwarfs knocked with their picks, extracting diamonds from a cave. It took me to my childhood, when I used to play with my older cousin's typewriter pretending to be a journalist. That night, I didn't write anything proper; I just contemplated my new machine before falling asleep.

The next day, I was ready to kick my writing. I put on my bathrobe, I prepared a big coffee and sat in the kitchen on my new chair in front of the Olivetti. Everything was set up for a great, compelling story, starring an empathic character who struggled to overcome the problems he encountered in an epic quest, or a dramatic story about the forbidden love of two characters coming from two different worlds. But again, I got nothing. Just the sound of the metallic bars of the typewriter falling on the paper, creating unconnected words that didn't lead to any phrase with sense.

I couldn't write. I couldn't focus. I didn't have any inspiration. The sound of the cars passing next to my apartment, the sirens of the ambulances, the people chatting in the bar downstairs... I needed a calmer place in order to get the best of my brain. I was too old to live in the city. I left my writing spot and sat on the sofa with my laptop to check a house for rent in the countryside.

The process was long. I visited lots of them. Some were too expensive, some too big, some too old, some too cold... After a long search, I finally found one that fit my expectations. It was just thirty minutes by car from the city.

It had a small living room with an American kitchen, and just one bedroom and a bathroom. I didn't need more. Besides, there was a window in the living room that led to big, plain fields. The perfect spot to put my desk.

I spent a whole week moving my belongings to my new place, and I made the whole house pretty cozy. But my favorite corner was the desk in front of the window with my Olivetti on it. I would write thousands of impressive pages from that place, and I would create the ultimate novel that I was aiming for.

But first, I would build a cellar inside the hut placed in my new garden, to store some wines and fine whiskeys. Because how could you become a best-selling writer without a good scotch next to your Olivetti?

PANIC

The fridge is empty, and the rubbish bags in the corridor stink. I am sweating and my head feels dizzy. I couldn't sleep last night thinking about this moment. I finally have to go out.

Preparation is key. I will leave at three, just after lunchtime, while people are still at home or in their offices. It is the hour that there are less people in the supermarkets and on the streets. I have my list of things I need to buy. Every time I go, I buy the same stuff, which lasts approximately sixteen days. Today it's Tuesday, so it should not be crowded outside. Mondays and Saturdays are the worst; I try to avoid them at all costs.

It's time to go out. I put on my gloves. I have my backpack filled with plastic bags and the shopping list in my pocket. I always give myself a minute or two in front of the door before going out, to reassure myself and calm down. But I never calm down. My hands shake, and my chest burns like a fireball spins in my stomach. I'm nauseous because of my anxiety and the stink of the rubbish.

One, two...three. I turn the keys and open the door. I take the stairs; I don't want to meet anybody in the elevator. My steps are fast and coordinated, like a sewing machine spinning thread.

"Good morning."

I almost have a heart attack. I didn't expect meeting a neighbor on the stairs. I lean against the wall so we can both pass without touching each other.

"Good morning," I moan, and I run away down the stairs.

I don't want to speak to him more.

Please, no more incidents today. The supermarket is just two minutes from my building. I throw away the three rubbish bags I am carrying, and I walk firmly to the store.

I have been coming to this supermarket for five years, and I know exactly the location of all the things I need to buy and the most efficient way to get to them.

Let's start with the coffee... Where is the coffee? It should be just on the left of the entrance door, and instead there are plastic dishes and cups and birthday candles... Oh, my God! They relocated all the products! I'm not going to make it in less than fifteen minutes.

Okay, breathe, don't panic. I hold my list in one hand, and I take a round through the whole supermarket, trying to grab all the items written on my list.

After having walked through all the aisles, I am missing half of the things I need. I have to get out of here; my breathing is getting faster, and I can feel the lack of oxygen in my lungs. But I can't find toilet paper, and I can't go back without toilet paper. I have to be brave and ask an employee.

"Excuse me," – my voice sounds shrill and trembling – "where is the toilet paper?"

"Third corridor on the right," she says, touching my arm, to which I react by stepping backwards and rushing to the toilet paper. This day is horrible.

I go to pay; this is the last moment that I need to interact with someone.

"Three plastic bags, please," I say, looking at the floor.

I pay with my credit card, I put all the groceries in the bags, and I go back to my apartment. My steps are long, and I can't think about anything else than closing my door with my key and finally being inside.

When I am just a few steps from the door, one plastic bag

breaks and tomatoes, oranges, and cans roll down the street. I hold the other two bags with my hands, and I don't know what to do. I am paralyzed. An old woman just passing by stops and takes some of the things that fell.

"I will help you," she says.

I can't stand it anymore. I leave the two bags I'm holding on the ground, and I sprint to my building. I get inside my apartment, and I close the door, turning my key three times.

PAIN

"Can you feel something?"

"Not really. No, no. I mean, I feel that you touch me, but no."

The tattooist carried on drawing the red dragon on my back, right on my scapula. The needle was perforating my skin at a high speed, and in the mirror, I could see a thin line of blood slipping down my back.

"It is impressive, you know?" he said while wiping my blood with a tissue. "It makes you a kind of superhero."

"For me, it's annoying. I actually don't like it."

"Why not?" he asked. "A lot of people have pain every day, and they would be delighted to be like you."

"I know, my mother takes a lot of painkillers for her lower back pain. But I can't feel it. I have been looking for pain during the last three years."

"Really? What did you do?" The tattooist stopped drawing to change the color of the ink. I used the pause to take a sip of juice.

"Well, I tried multiple methods. To be honest, I didn't have much expectation with this one."

"Wait, wait... What do you mean, multiple methods?"

"It means that I tried to feel pain in a lot of manners. I don't want to give you more details."

The tattooist looked impressed by my words. But I didn't want to share what I did to try to feel pain; it made me feel ashamed and uncomfortable. Once, I let my friends hit my balls with a baseball bat. I ended up in the hospital, I had to have surgery, and I almost lost one of my testicles. I burned my arm with a lighter until my skin melted completely. My body was a map full of scars.

"Have you always been like this?" he asked.

"Yes. Of course, when you're a child, you don't know that you don't feel pain. You see other children crying after falling on the floor, and you don't understand it. You feel that you're different, but you don't know why."

"Have you ever broken a bone?"

"I broke my arm when I was seven. I didn't realize that I broke it, I just couldn't move my hand, and I saw that half of my arm was falling and couldn't stay still. It was at school, during break. When the teacher saw it after a few minutes, she almost fainted."

I was reminded of those situations when my parents got scared by my accidents, and I couldn't understand what was going on.

"Well, that is impressive," he repeated. "So you don't feel physical pain, but do you feel emotional pain?"

"What do you mean?"

"When someone does something bad to you, something that is painful, do you feel it?"

I remained in silence for a few seconds. I had never thought about it. It was true that people commented things like, "It was painful that you didn't call me on my birthday" or "I felt pain when my grandfather died."

"I don't know," I said. "I have been sad, and stressed. But I don't know what it's like to feel emotional pain."

"Nobody ever betrayed you?"

"My ex-girlfriend cheated on me with a friend, and I broke up with her. I was sad, but it was not a hard moment for me. I was just sad, in the same way I can be sad now because of the fact that I can't feel any pain."

"Wow, you're kind of an alien. And what do you feel when you see someone in pain, someone who is suffering?"

I was enjoying the conversation with the tattooist so much. Very few people had been interested in the fact that I couldn't feel any pain, and I always felt alone with my peculiarity.

"I'm jealous," I answered. "I feel I would like to be in their place."

"Can you feel the pain through others?" Another pause to change the ink. That was it. I could try to feel the pain through another's pain and suffering.

"I haven't tried yet."

He smiled at me. After ten minutes, he finished his job. A long red dragon spitting fire from his mouth with a sword piercing his heart.

I spent the next six months recognizing pain through others. I spent hours in emergency rooms in hospitals witnessing how other patients had pain. I assisted in several bullfighting squares, where the bull suffered from a heartless man who killed it slowly and the public shouted joyfully. I went to oncology group therapy, where patients and families explained their suffering related to the uncertainty of an inevitable death. And I comprehended pain. And I was grateful to not be able to feel it under my skin.

CRUSH

Pedro was doing the daily crossword when she arrived. He was sitting in his chair, the same one he had been sitting in every single morning the last ten years. A routine he wasn't eager to change.

His big prostate forced him to stand to pee. The retirement home had big spaces for the residents, and the main room had big windows from where you could see a perfect skyline of Barcelona. But the toilets were small. Pedro always complained about their size and the fact that they didn't have any lock inside. The nurses said it was for security reasons.

Pedro came back from the toilet and was startled. The new resident who just arrived that morning was sitting in his place.

"Ehem... Excuse me, madam," he said, "this is my place. As you can see, I was doing the crossword."

"Hello, dear. Oh, it's okay. There are a lot of chairs in this room. You can take your crossword."

She didn't move. Pedro was fuming, but he wanted to be polite.

"Maybe you could change your place..." he said. "You know, I always sit in this exact place in the mornings, and I do my crossword. Every day. Here. In this place."

"Today, it will be the first day you will do your crossword in another place. I like this chair; the view is fantastic, and the sun shines nicely. My name is María."

María smiled at him. She had beautiful white teeth, probably dentures, but it was difficult to say. She had shiny gray straight hair, and her skin looked like she wasn't the right age to be in a retirement home.

"Nice to meet you, María. I'm Pedro."

Pedro took the crossword and sat on a chair a few meters from María. He was angry at himself for having let the new resident take his place. He gazed at her; she was staring at him, drawing a perfect, playful smile. She was beautiful.

Pedro had been living in the retirement home for ten years already. He had worked as a real estate agent, and he had enough savings to afford a quiet and calm retirement. He didn't have any good friends in the retirement home, but he was well known and respected.

He began to be friends with María. Pedro woke up early every morning and ate his breakfast quickly to get his place in the common room. But when he stood to pee, María would take his place. This irritated Pedro, but at the same time, he found it funny.

"Why did you come here?" Pedro asked María.

"Here, where? In the retirement home?" María said.

"Yes."

"My two sons wanted me to be in a safe and calm place... Well, they're too busy to care for me. But I don't need to be cared for! I can do everything by myself. So basically they put me in this prison against my will."

"This is not a prison," said Pedro. "We can go out if we want. And it has a nice garden, a beautiful view, the food is good..."

"A prison with a nice garden, a beautiful view, and good food. But a prison after all."

Pedro and María spent a lot of time together. They sat at the same table during meals and strolled in the garden in the afternoons. For Pedro, it was the first time he had such contact with another resident. He was happier than ever and, though he didn't want to admit it, he started to develop feelings for

María. One evening after dinner, María took Pedro aside in the common room.

"Pedro, I have an idea."

"I'm already shaking. What are you proposing?"

"I would like to go to the coast. Next to the beach. I want to go tonight."

"Tonight? And how? We shouldn't go out at night, and there are no taxis in this area."

"Let's meet in the women's bathroom in the common room in one hour. Prepare a bag with your medications and some clothes."

Pedro packed and stood next to the door of his room. He debated whether to go or not. Even though it was not forbidden, they were not supposed to leave the building at night. Besides, he didn't know how they would get to the beach. His heart beat fast, and he was sweating. He felt his adrenaline being discharged from his back. He was excited about that kind of date with María.

Pedro waited outside the women's bathroom as María had told him. Ten minutes, and she hadn't appeared. He felt disappointed, and he thought that she had just played with him.

"Psst! Pedro!" a voice from inside the restroom whispered. "What are you doing here?"

"I thought that we would meet outside the bathroom."

"I said inside! I was waiting for so long," said María. "Never mind, come here, quick!"

María held Pedro by his hand and took him inside.

"We have to jump through the window," said María.

"Through the window? How?"

"Climb on the toilet and jump. The window faces directly outside the building."

Pedro used all his strength to climb, and he jumped outside. He thought of how easy it would have been thirty years before.

María jumped after him.

"How are we going to go to the coast?" asked Pedro.

"Look."

María took car keys out of her pocket and pressed the button. The lights of a gray Volkswagen Golf parked fifteen meters behind them turned on. María ran and sat in the passenger seat.

"Oh, do I need to drive?" asked Pedro. "I have not driven a car in ten years."

"Yes, I don't have a driving license."

"What? And how-"

"There is no time to talk. Quick, drive before they get us!"

Pedro turned on the car. He stalled the car a couple of times, and he crashed into the car parked behind them, to which María reacted with a loud laugh.

"Where are we going?" asked Peter.

"To Lloret de Mar."

"That's more than one and a half hours from Barcelona!"

"Never mind, we have the whole night."

María turned on the radio and selected a rock station. 'Rockaway Beach' by Ramones was playing. Pedro felt scared and excited at the same time. The back pain he used to have felt like tickles in that moment.

"Why do you have a car if you don't have a driving license?" asked Pedro.

"This is not my car. I took the keys from the night shift nurse."

"What? I'm driving a stolen car! We have to go back."

"Come on, Pedro! Let's have some fun. We'll give it back tomorrow."

Pedro hesitated, but he kept driving. He was thrilled, and he didn't want to ruin the night.

They got to Lloret de Mar after two hours. They parked

on the beach promenade. Pedro couldn't hold his bladder and peed just next to the car. María laughed at Pedro. She got out of the car and opened her arms. Pedro hadn't noticed how elegant she dressed that night until then.

They went first to the casino. Pedro lost count of how many cocktails they drank there. Lights, music, people laughing and cheering... He didn't know if they were winning or losing, he just knew that he was having the time of his life.

María proposed they go dancing. They went to a nightclub where the reggaeton music was so loud that Pedro could hear the beat even with his half deafness. He moved his body like he didn't have a titanium prosthetic in his hips. They danced until 4 a.m. when, both feeling exhausted, they found a cheap hostel where they could spend the night.

The place was dirty, and the owner received them while smoking a cigarette. They got a private room with two beds. Music and loud moans were audible from the corridor, and an intense smell of weed emanated from some rooms. Pedro and María fell asleep quickly after a night of joy.

Pedro woke up with a huge hangover. María was already awake, washing her face in the dirty bathroom.

"This place is awful," said Pedro.

"Good morning to you too, darling."

"I have the worst hangover ever."

"Let's get some breakfast, then!"

They left the hostel and ambled to the beach promenade. The sun was already high, and Pedro sweat all the alcohol he drank last night.

They sat on the terrace of a small beach bar. Pedro was as hungry as a crocodile. They ordered crepes and ice cream and two coffees.

"We should go back to the retirement home now," said Pedro. "They might be worried about us."

"Not yet. We can have a nice day on the beach. It's so sunny today."

"And what about the car? Surely they already called the police."

"We'll come up with something, don't worry."

They had an awkward silence for the first time since they left Barcelona. Pedro didn't feel comfortable being out of the retirement home for so long, but he was even more panicked about the stolen car.

"I'll go pay the bill," said Pedro while taking out his wallet. "Oh, shit, I don't have any cash! Do you have anything?"

María checked her purse; it was also empty.

"What are we going to do?" asked Pedro. "I don't have a credit card, I forgot it in Barcelona!"

"Come!"

María took Pedro by the arm and almost made him fall on the floor. They trotted away from the restaurant. After fifty meters, they turned the corner.

"My heart is going to explode!" said Pedro. "This is the second crime I've committed in twenty-four hours!"

They both laughed aloud. It was that kind of laugh where you lose your surroundings, where you can barely breathe, and if you are an elderly person, you pee a little in your underwear.

They came back to the car and realized they were running out of gas.

"We're not going to reach Barcelona. We need to stop at a gas station, but we don't have any cash," said Pedro.

"Don't panic, Pedro. We'll figure out how to pay."

They stopped at a lonely gas station out of town surrounded just by fields. There was nobody there, just a guy inside the store. The heat of midday would boil a pot of water and melt a golden statue. A black Mercedes Benz stopped to get some gas. An old guy with brown skin and thin sunglasses took the pump to fill his car. He was alone.

"Pedro, this is our opportunity. You go to his car and take his wallet; he'll have it in the driver-side door. I'll distract him."

"What?"

María had already left the car and was heading toward the guy, leaving Pedro with words in his mouth. María unfastened the upper button of her blouse and shook her hair with both hands. She stood in front of the old man and chatted with him next to the pump. The old man looked very interested in what María was explaining. Pedro nipped to the Mercedes until he was just one meter behind the man. María held the old man's hand and let him kiss her hand. Pedro felt jealous of him, and he hated him instantly. He found the wallet and put it in his trousers and went back to the car. María came after a few seconds.

"Run, run!" she said, while Pedro turned on the car and rushed out of the gas station. "We are the Bonnie and Clyde of the third age!"

They escaped quickly from the gas station, driving as if they were in a rally.

"What did you say to that man?" asked Pedro.

"Oh, nothing. Just a little flirting."

"You could have been more subtle."

"Pedro, please. I'm seventy-four! You are not my father."

"I'm just saying that we could have gotten the same result without the flirting."

"Oh, I see... You're jealous."

"No, I'm not." Pedro's face flushed.

"Hahaha! Yes, you are jealous of that man. Hahaha!"

María laughed and Pedro stayed silent, his face red like a tomato.

They stopped at another gas station and filled the car using the cash they stole from the old man. He was a wealthy person, or at least his wallet said so.

They drove back in the direction of Barcelona. Pedro was

reminded the night before. It was the best time of his life.

"María, it was such a funny night."

"Oh yes, you bet it was. I hadn't felt as alive in a very long time. Thank you, Pedro."

Pedro was flattered by María's comment. It was 4 p.m., and he didn't want to go back to Barcelona. Out of the blue, he pushed the brake of the car and made a U-turn.

"What are you doing?" María shouted. "Do you wanna kill us?"

"We have plenty of cash in that wallet. It would be such a pity not to use it. We're driving north to the coast."

Pedro saw María's eyes shining with emotion, and she gave him a huge smile.

They took a curved secondary road that went through cliffs next to the sea. They talked about their past. Pedro explained that he had been sixty when his wife died. He wasn't very happy with her, but he hadn't met any other woman after. María divorced when her two sons were very young. They moved to France for ten years, and then they came back to Barcelona. She never got married again either.

They drove for three hours, stopping in small coves to rest and put their feet in the water.

"I would like to visit Greece," said María.

"Why Greece? It might be similar to here, I guess."

"I was fascinated by Greek mythology as a child. Stories of gods that mingle with humans and punish people for eternity."

"Greece is far. I have never been out of Spain."

Pedro felt like a couple of teenagers dating for the first time. They had conversations about the purpose of life, the future, their experiences... And he had tickles in the stomach every time María looked at him and smiled.

The day was reaching its end, and twilight made the sea turn first silver and then pink, creating a dance of colors that moved every second. They stopped in a fancy hotel located on a cliff. They didn't mind the cost, as their trip was funded by the old man with the Mercedes Benz.

The lobby guy took their bags to the room. They went directly to the garden of the hotel for a walk. Next to the swimming pool, there was a marvelous view of the sea, with the full moon reflecting on the water and the stars shining in the sky. They sat on the grass.

"María... This has been the best time of my life. I hope that this is real and I'm not in a dream."

"Everything is real, Pedro."

They kissed for the first time, like a young couple who were just discovering what love was. Pedro hugged María, and she put her hand in his trousers.

"María... I don't have any Viagra," said Pedro.

"Don't worry, Pedro. Do what you can."

They had sex next to the swimming pool. They melted into one body, and the stars clapped over their heads while the waves crashed on the cliff.

"Ehem... Excuse me." They heard a voice coming from behind them. It was the lobby guy. "It is not allowed... It is not allowed to be naked in the gardens. I tried to apprise you, but apparently you didn't hear me. A family just complained."

"Oh, sorry," said Pedro. "I'm half deaf. As you see, I am seventy-eight. And I just had sex."

Pedro and María laughed, and the lobby guy went back inside the hotel. They lay for a few moments in silence, staring at the stars.

"Pedro, I need to tell you something."

"More surprises? I don't know if I'm ready."

María looked at Pedro in the eyes. "I'm ill," she said.

"What do you mean, you're ill?"

"I have lung cancer. I already did one treatment of

chemotherapy, but it was not effective. They proposed me to do another treatment, but I denied. I wanted to live the last moments of my life without feeling sick all the time. That's why my sons put me in the retirement home."

"Wow... I understand." Pedro took María's hand. "You are not made for staying in a retirement home."

María smiled and a tear dropped. It was the first time that Pedro felt that she was vulnerable. He hugged her.

"Tomorrow, we'll drive through the coast. We'll go to Greece."

"I love you, Pedro."

Their arms linked like creeper plants, and María leaned her head on Pedro's chest. Their hearts beat in unison, celebrating the beginning of a new life.

SHEPHERD

Patrick opened his eyes with the first sunlight. The night had been hard; it rained almost four hours in a row and the cartons where he lay become wet. Today, he would have to go in search of a new bed. He checked the wine bottle lying next to him, and after shaking it, he poured the few drops left into his mouth.

The day was gray, and even though it was late spring, the humidity nailed into his bones like poisoned spikes. From the number of pedestrians and their lack of rushing, Patrick guessed that it was Sunday. Most of the supermarkets would be closed, so he would have to go to the bazaar if he would like some wine.

As always, he sat on his corner for one or two hours after waking up before he would finally stand to stretch his legs. He spotted a guy standing twenty meters from him, staring at him motionless. He wore a black suit and a fedora hat, and even though Patrick's poor sight didn't allow him to focus well on his face, he noticed a curly ginger hair under his hat. Patrick felt frequently disturbed when people watched him, except with kids. When someone gazed at him for what he considered was too long, in the best of cases he, would stick his tongue out, or more often, he would show his middle finger and shout to whoever he thought was observing him.

Patrick first waved at the guy, and when he didn't receive any answer, he threatened him to come closer, moving his hand in a provocative way. No response.

"You fucker! What are you looking at?"

No answer. Patrick took his belongings – a backpack, a

blanket, and a shopping cart he used to move his personal possessions – with the intention of approaching the guy. When he turned his head, he had disappeared.

Patrick went to the social lunchroom to get some food and headed to the bazaar for wine. He used the last coins he had left. While he was sitting at his spot drinking his wine, he saw the same man again, staring at him. His face looked familiar to him. He had the strange feeling of having seen him before, like he was a part of him for a long time, maybe in this life or maybe in another.

Patrick sprinted to him, struggling to not fall on the floor after the effects of alcohol.

"Are you looking for a problem?" he shouted. "Why are you spying on me?"

"Sorry, sir. I don't want any problems. I just thought that you could change your spot."

"You want me to change my place? Bullshit! I have been sleeping in this place for five years! I am not changing my spot because an ass-kisser bastard in a suit says so!"

"I am sorry to bother you, sir."

The man in the suit walked away while Patrick was still shouting at him and spitting.

The rest of the day turned out to be a normal Sunday for Patrick. He hid from the rain in his usual spot, drinking wine and thinking about what the man in the suit had said to him. The rain was getting stronger, and Patrick was already concerned about having to withstand one more rainy night. *Why did he tell me to move?* he thought. *I am good here, partly covered from the rain, and I have always been in this spot.* But something from inside pushed him to change his location. When he had just one bottle of wine left, he took his belongings and moved under the outdoor stairs of the train station. It was a comfortable corner, more sheltered than the spot he was in before and more covered from the rain. It rained the whole night, but Patrick slept without even noticing.

He woke up with a hangover and drank the last drops of wine he had left. When it stopped raining, Patrick took his things and moved to his usual spot. He was astonished when he got there. Four policemen surrounded the area, and a "no trespassing" plastic band restricted the presence of pedestrians. The small ceiling that usually covered Patrick had collapsed because of the rain, and a pile of debris laid in the place where he used to sleep.

"What the fuck is this?" he shouted.

"Excuse me, sir, you cannot pass this line."

"This is my place, I live here!"

Patrick couldn't believe it. *How the hell did that man know what was going to happen?* he thought. The policemen didn't pay any attention to him, and Patrick felt like an invisible person.

He ambled around the station with no destination. After going to social services and receiving his poor weekly pay, he went to buy some wine and sat on the other side of the station, from where he could see the workers clearing the ruins. *If I had stayed there last night, I would have died.* Patrick couldn't stop thinking about it.

Then he saw him again. From a distance, the man in the suit peered at him, still. Patrick ran to him, leaving all his belongings. The man didn't move.

"How did you know that the ceiling would collapse?"

"I don't know what you're talking about, sir," the man in the suit answered.

"Why did you tell me to move from my place?"

"I just thought that with the rain, you could find a better place to stay."

"You motherfucker!" Patrick was furious.

"I think you should go for a walk in the park next to the

station today, it's very relaxing."

"Don't tell me what to do!"

Patrick had a look around; a bunch of pedestrians observed him shouting with scared faces.

"And what are you looking at?" he shouted. "Do I have monkeys on my face?"

The people moved away quickly. Patrick turned his head to keep talking with the man in the suit.

"And you…"

There was no sign of the man in the suit. He fled.

Patrick took his belongings and headed to the park. It was finally sunny after the last few cloudy days. The park had a peculiar mixed smell of spring pollen and dog pee. It had a small artificial lake that contained several empty beer cans and some plastic bags, where a couple of ducks swam and ate the rest of the human food.

What am I supposed to do in here? Patrick wondered. He reminded himself that the first couple of nights after he arrived in the city, he slept in the park. He went to visit his old spot where he used to stay, a bench next to a small building that was used as a storage room for the park cleaners. He sat on the bench and looked around. The fresh grass grew with the spring, forming a perfect shiny green carpet, and the trees were flourishing, with the background sound of the melodies of birds. Patrick dropped his bottle of wine by accident. When he crouched, he saw a red wallet on the ground. It contained fifty euros inside. Patrick hadn't possessed that amount of money in a long time. *I am going to buy whiskey today,* he thought.

He slept the following night in his new spot under the stairs outside the station. He felt grateful for the guy in the suit for having suggested he change his location, and he still wondered where he had seen his face before. He spent the next few days looking for him, walking in the middle of the pedestrians, chasing people in suits.

Finally, he saw him. The man in the suit was standing still, peering at him again. Patrick ran to him.

"I have been looking for you for so long! Thank you for your advice!" said Patrick.

"You are welcome, sir."

"Now tell me what to do."

"I am not a counselor, sir."

"I said, you tell me what to do!" Patrick shouted. Some pedestrians already stopped and stared at Patrick.

"If you want advice, sir, I recommend you stop drinking."

"Bullshit! I'm not stopping drinking! Tell me, where can I find a wallet? Or some money?"

"Sir, I don't know..."

"Tell me, motherfucker!"

Patrick was out of his mind and moved in a threatening way toward the man in the suit, shouting in rage. He was surrounded by pedestrians when four policemen and three paramedics came to take him.

"What are you doing, fuckers?" said Patrick.

Patrick struggled to not get caught, but there were six people against him, and he was alone and drunk. Patrick moved his eyes to find the man in the suit, but he had vanished. Next thing Patrick noticed was being inside an ambulance taking him to a hospital.

THIRST

Lisa moved from speculation to suspicion after randomly seeing Martin's car parked next to the train station. What was he doing there? He was supposed to be at work at that time. She felt awkward and didn't want to get closer to the car, in case Martin was around. What would she say if he saw her examining the car? *I was just spying on you?* No, this was a bad idea. She would just slide an innocent question at home later.

They had been married already six years, but they had been together for almost nine years, and now they lived in the suburbs, in a semidetached house with a backyard that they called home. Lisa always considered themselves as a joyous couple. But there were some things that didn't look as idyllic during the last few months. Lisa noticed that Martin was absent and avoided conversations with her. He didn't even look at her eyes while sitting at dinner. He also spent so much time on the phone and came home later from work every day. She was sad. And she felt guilty.

Martin came back late from work, as usual.

"Hi, honey! How was work?" Lisa smiled to him, hoping that the question sounded natural and naive.

"Oh, I am exhausted. I spent the whole afternoon with a client. In these days of recession, it is very difficult to get a good deal..."

Lisa didn't pay attention to his explanations. She just wondered how to ask him why he had the car parked next to the train station. Martin took off his jacket and passed by her.

"I have an afternoon meeting tomorrow in London. I'll probably stay the night."

"You could come back on the last train. You won't finish after ten, right?"

"I don't know, but I might be tired, and I prefer to stay the night there. Besides, I have another meeting in London as well the following morning."

"You're spending more time out of the house every day, Martin. What about me?"

"Honey, we will soon close a good deal, which will bring us lots of benefits. Then I will be freer and have more time for us." Martin closed the bathroom door behind him, leaving Lisa with words in her mouth.

After buying a wig and sunglasses in the bazaar, Lisa went back to the train station the next morning. She was ashamed of what she was doing, but she wanted to know the truth. She waited four hours until Martin's car came to the parking lot. She observed how he moved from a distance, and he didn't look like he would be afraid of Lisa spying on him. Lisa followed him inside the train, and she sat in the same carriage a few seats behind him.

She realized she didn't have any plan. What if Martin saw her? She would not have any excuse. And what would she do when she found out who he was meeting? Lisa was overwhelmed. She recognized that she had gone very far and considered the possibility that she was too paranoid and all her thoughts of infidelity were just made up by her mind.

Martin stood from his seat and turned in Lisa's direction. Lisa's heart rate was as fast as the train. She started to sweat and put all her effort on trying to not throw up. She hid herself by staring out the window, and she could see in the reflection of the glass how Martin passed next to her without even noticing her. She put herself together and stood some meters away from Martin.

He got out at Euston Station. Lisa was struggling to not lose Martin in the crowd while trying to keep a secure distance in case he turned his head.

She wondered why he was cheating on her. They had a wonderful life, and they had had a good relationship for a very long time. It was just one thing that was not working well, and Lisa was consciously avoiding thinking about it.

Martin wanted children. And Lisa wanted children as well. But they still hadn't succeeded, and they had been trying already for three years. The medical tests they had done didn't show any abnormalities, and all the doctors they visited said to keep trying, but there were no results. Lisa felt guilty about it. Was Martin looking for another woman to have children with? That thought terrified Lisa the most. She could handle an affair with a young lady, followed by a few weeks of arguments, and finally keep going on as a good wife and husband as if nothing had happened. But she would not stand it if he had children with another woman.

It was getting dark, and Martin was still walking. It had been about one hour since they left the station, and Lisa wondered why he didn't take a taxi. Martin turned into a small alley and stopped in front of a door. He peered at both sides of the street, which forced Lisa to hide herself in a quick move behind a garbage can. She kept her head behind the garbage for a few seconds, and she didn't spot Martin. Lisa strode to the door where Martin had been standing. It was a small metallic door, with no written sign outside and without any bell to ring. What was this place? It didn't look like a good dating spot.

"Are you coming in?" A voice from behind Lisa startled her. It was a fifty-year-old man in a long green coat.

"Yes," Lisa answered without having thought what she was doing there. The man passed by Lisa and knocked on the door with a specific rhythm. Someone opened after few seconds. He wore a long black robe with a dark gray hood and a white, inexpressive mask. The guy who knocked on the door passed first and went down a long corridor. The man in the mask stared at Lisa.

"I see that you're new. What is your name?"

"Yes... My name is Laura," she lied.

"Who invited you?"

"Martin...Martin Harris."

"Welcome, Laura. Here you have your clothes. The room is at the end of the corridor. We will start in ten minutes."

"Thank you."

Lisa put on the dress, the hood, and the mask. She clumped through a long stone corridor that smelled so musty that she was close to fainting. The dim lightbulbs hanging from the low ceiling barely made the cobblestone floor visible. Lisa was frightened, but there was no way back. She asked herself if she was really stalking her husband or if she just followed a stranger by mistake into a wrong place. At that point, she wished she had stayed at home pretending that nothing wrong was happening. An oak door with a golden latch stood at the end of the long corridor. Lisa hesitated before opening it. Her chest was growing so tight it became hard to breathe, and a wave of acid welled up in her belly.

Inside the room, there were about fifteen people forming a semi-circle and waiting in silence, all of them dressed in the black robe, the dark gray hood, and the white, inexpressive mask. The room was old and dark, and the damp odor from the corridor was even stronger. Some stone columns stood in the room, placed almost randomly, like they would like to imitate a Nordic forest. Lisa placed herself next to another person from the circle and remained silent. She tried unsuccessfully to identify Martin through the holes of the mask.

After a few minutes, someone came through the door. He wore a red robe with a hood and a golden mask.

"Good evening, siblings. Today, we have a very fresh one. Twenty-three years old." A muttering of approbation came from the rest of the participants. Two people emerged from a dark corner of the room. They were dragging a young naked guy. He was unconscious and pale, but still breathing. They placed him in the center of the room, and they joined the circle. The guy with the red robe and the golden mask stepped in front. He babbled some incomprehensible words, and swiftly, he took a knife from his sleeve and cut the guy's throat in a smooth move. Lisa wanted to scream, but the sounds were not emanating from her mouth. The guy in the red robe got on his knees, pushed his mask up, and gulped the blood that was flowing from the throat. One by one, the participants imitated the same action.

Lisa was completely paralyzed. She glanced around, not able to focus on what was happening in her surroundings. Then she saw him. The unmistakable square-shaped chin of Martin with two days' gray beard, swallowing the blood like a wolf that had been starving for two months. She then realized she was the only one standing. Lisa got on her knees, pushed her mask up and placed her tongue on a stream of blood flowing from the guy's belly. She felt a sharp metallic taste on her lips and a fresh, pleasant scent rising from her nose to her brain. She felt inebriated by the fresh essence of the blood. Once she started, she couldn't stop until there was no more blood to drain.

The red robed guy stood.

"We will communicate with you by the usual method as soon as we have the next one. Now you can go."

People left one by one through the door. Lisa had lost Martin in the crowd long ago, but she didn't care. From now on, she would follow him to his late-night work.

POSSESS

When I look at it, it waves back. It is a mutual love, I know it. Relationships are not limited to interpersonal connection, nor to person-animal alliance. Some people are in love with pieces of art, for example, even though a piece of art will never react to them; it is just unidirectional love. People are in love with objects, with things that they exchange for money, things as impersonal as cars or fancy bags. Pathetic. Me, I am in love with the Sun.

But I am not an average Sun lover, one of those folks who lay down on the grass under the Sun until they burn and their skin becomes irregular like the peel of a rotten orange. My love for the Sun is real, something mystic and visceral. I have an authentic connection with the Sun, I can communicate with it somehow, but I am not able to explain how it works.

A considerable amount of people don't deserve the Sun, either because they don't appreciate it or because they are not grateful enough for it. Some of them even abuse the Sun, with solar panels or huge plantations that depend totally on the light of the Sun, but they just benefit the ones who own them. You won't have any slaves, will you? So why do you need to have the Sun as your slave? Totally disrespectful.

Because of those senseless people who don't care about the Sun and take profit off it, I need to find a solution. I want the Sun for myself.

I walk through the deep forest, under the shadow that the tall pines provide, smelling the scents of humid leaves and fresh mud. My heart beats like hooves stepping on the ground during a stampede. I am heading to the Dowager. People call her the Dowager because she is said to have the honor of being the widow of the Devil himself. I always heard this story from my parents and my grandparents, who heard about it from their parents and grandparents.

Nowadays very few people believe in the existence of the Dowager, but the inhabitants of the region will avoid hiking in this area. People will not admit it, but they are still afraid of the Dowager, like a child who strongly tries to sleep during Christmas night knowing that Santa is not real.

I do believe that the Dowager exists. As a child, a cousin of a friend from school got lost in the forest. The organization of the whole town to look for him was futile. His body simply vanished. Some said the Dowager took him, others said that he fell off a cliff and vultures ate him.

Never mind, I am not thinking about the dangers of the Dowager. I am willing to take the risk. My duty is imperative.

The forest is getting denser, and there isn't a clear path to follow. I have been walking for more than four hours, and the midday spring warmth and humidity make it difficult to advance faster. I feel that the air is heavier, thicker, and it flows with difficulties to fill my lungs. I have not heard any bird chirping for more than ten minutes. There is something around, I can feel it. I cannot be far from the Dowager.

An intense odor mixed of curium and sulfur impregnates the fresh air in the forest. My vision blurs, and my eyes are itchy, which makes me falter.

"Be careful with what-t-t you desire," a creepy voice echoes. I can't tell from which direction it comes. I feel completely disoriented. But I don't panic.

"Are you the Dowager?"

No answer. Just this heat and stink, which makes me feel

dazed. I take some steps, staggering, not really knowing where I am treading. I can barely see a meter in front of me.

"Where are you, Dowager? I don't fear you."

A warm blast of wind passes behind me, leaving a moist stench.

"I know what-t you want-t-t-t..." says the Dowager. "You are greedy and possessive, just-t like me."

"Can you give me what I want?" My voice reverberates in my head.

"I can give you what-t you want-t-t... But-t-t do I want-t to give it-t to you?" The Dowager's voice is as hypnotizing as her odor. I can't move my feet from the ground; it feels like they were made of two huge rocks of five tons each. I am thirsty.

"Do you know why I married the Devil?" she asks.

"I don't know."

"I wanted to be warm. I wanted to be the warmest-t-t person in the world. Back then, the winters were freezing, and the only way we had to warm ourselves was the fire. But-t-t not-t everybody was able to possess the fire..."

The Dowager talks in a slow pace, like she would like to curve time with her tempo. And it works – I have no idea for how long I stand in the same position. I don't know if it is still daylight. Or is it already tomorrow?

"I wanted the fire just-t-t for myself. For me, and for nobody else. I dug underground until I met the Devil. I seduced him, and I married him. He lived in the fire, so I could have as much as I desired. But-t-t soon I realized I wanted more. I didn't-t love the Devil, and I didn't-t-t want-t to share the fire with Him."

The story the Dowager explains keeps me awake; I want to know where she is heading. Otherwise, I would have already fainted a long time ago.

"One night-t-t," continues the Dowager, "when He was sleeping, I went-t-t up to the surface, and I took a huge silver stake. Without-t-t hesitating, I stabbed it-t-t into His chest-t-t. A massive explosion propelled me back to the surface, creating an enormous volcano. There was no trace of the Devil. From that-t-t moment-t, I am the only one who owns the fire. I am the fire."

I am getting used to the heat and stink, but I still can't see properly. I don't have any idea what the Dowager looks like. I imagine an old woman burning in fire, maybe with a snake tongue, or maybe with huge blazing antlers on her head. But she could have every shape, or no shape at all.

"I will give you what-t-t you want-t-t. But-t you have to know that-t-t nothing will ever be the same again. Is it-t really what-t-t you desire?"

"I came here for it. Give it to me," I say.

"Determined and greedy boy... I like it-t-t-t. I will give you the power of the Sun...just-t-t for you. The light-t and the flames, the warmth and the life."

A colossal flare surrounds me, making an extreme heat that would ignite the moon. A sparkle leaves everything white and blinds me for a few seconds, until I am finally able to see through it. I am burning, but I don't melt, I am blinding, but I am not sightless. Now the whole world lies under eternal darkness. I have all the light. I am the Sun.

WHIMS

In the olden days, when the rivers were clean and the air was fresh, the unicorns were real and the knights were gentle, there was a beautiful little princess living in a palace with her father the King and her mother the Queen, in an idyllic valley surrounded by high mountains. The palace was located on a small hill, and it had the shiniest walls and the prettiest towers. Down in the valley, there was a tiny village with white, rocky houses where the villagers lived in joy and peace. The village was ringed by deep green fields, and a river with clear, cold water was used by the villagers to fish and clean their clothes.

The princess lived in abundance. As she had no siblings, she had everything she desired. Once, for her birthday, she ordered two hundred fifty cakes made from blueberries and cottage cheese. The whole village participated in her extravagant present, putting in all their effort and skills. But she missed one thing: happiness. And she was desperately looking for it.

The impossibility of finding happiness, even with all her whims fulfilled, was the reason for her escape. On a warm full moon night of summer, when the princess was about to turn fourteen years old, she took a carriage from the palace and filled it with gold and groceries. She dressed herself as a villager and ran away from the valley.

The first thing she had in mind when thinking about happiness was love. But not a usual love, it had to be the love of a prince. And not any no-name-chunky-regular prince; it had to be a handsome, charming, ideal prince. So, she visited many villages, all of them with their pretty palace where a prince awaited a beautiful princess to delight him. None of them was the handsome, charming, ideal prince she was looking for. Some of them were definitely handsome, others were charming, others were rich, others were strong. But they were all boring and pedant. They tried to impress her with empty words and an abundance of food and astonishing views from the tower of the palace. She already had all those things in her palace. After more than twenty unsuccessful dates, she realized that the love of a prince was not the thing that would make her happy.

The princess always enjoyed perfumes. In her valley, perfumes were an exclusive good due to the lack of resources to produce them. The princess thought that if she had the most exotic and expensive perfumes, she would be happy. She asked in every perfume store in every village where she could get the best fragrances, and the answer was always the same: "the old lady living next to the swamp." Nobody knew exactly where she lived, and very few people had seen her, but they all agreed that she was unique. So the princess headed in the direction of the swamp. The closer she got to the water, the denser the fog became, and the feeling of loneliness got more intense. It was dark night when she arrived next to the swamp. The water was black and stinky, there was no sign of any animal nearby. But the princess had the creepy feeling of being observed.

"Hello, Princess."

"Who are you? Where are you?" asked the princess with a shaking voice.

"I am the lady you are looking for. I am the queen of fragrances, the chief of smells, the master of perfumes."

An old lady showed herself from the fog. She wore a black hood and carried an oil lamp in her hand.

"I know why you came to see me," said the old lady with

an eerie voice. "I will give you my best perfumes, but this is not the place where you will find what you are looking for."

"How do you know what I'm looking for?"

"I can see it in your eyes. Look through other people's eyes, and you will find it."

The old lady approached the princess and handed her a bag full of small glass bottles. The princess glanced at the interior of the bag and saw all those perfumes. A brief electric feeling coursed through her body. When she raised her head, the old lady had disappeared. She took one perfume, smelled it, and poured a little on her neck. What a fantastic fragrance. She got a dizzy feeling, like she was flying. She thought for a moment that she was happy. But in the same way the perfume lost its intensity, so did that happiness fade. The princess felt hopeless. Neither the love of a prince nor the most exotic perfumes made her happy. But it was one thing the princess always desired and never had. As a child, she used to sneak into her mother's room and take some of her jewelry; it made her feel like an adult and pretty. She knew exactly where to go.

Not far from her village, there was a jeweler who was said to be the best in all the region. He had the cleanest gold and the biggest and shiniest diamonds. The princess drove her carriage to the jeweler's house. It took her three days and three nights to get there. She was so excited about the idea of owning hundreds of jewels that she almost didn't sleep. She got there early in the morning of a hot and sunny day. The jeweler was working in the back. He was a short old man with gray hair and a massive mustache.

"Good morning, young lady," said the jeweler, "are you looking for something particular?"

"I would like to see your jewelry," said the princess.

The jeweler took a wooden trunk and opened it in front of the princess. The contents were so shiny that the princess had to cover her eyes. She took some of the artistic jewels out of the trunk. There were bracelets, anklets, tiaras, earrings, necklaces, rings... They were the prettiest jewels she had ever seen.

"Would you like to buy something, young lady?"

"I want all of them."

The princess showed all her gold, and the jeweler agreed to sell all the jewelry he had stored.

The princess took the jewelry with both her hands and lay in the middle of a green field to hug her precious new acquisitions. She felt warmth in her body, and she started to laugh loudly. Her skin was full of goosebumps. She thought that with all this jewelry, she would be happy forever. But as the hours passed, the feeling of excitement and joy vanished.

After one day, the princess felt exactly the same way she felt before starting her trip. Angry at herself, disappointed and in a fit of rage, she threw all her jewelry in the middle of the field. Exhausted, she sat on a tree trunk and cried in silence. She lost all hope of ever being happy.

Meanwhile, a young farmer who was working on the field passed through the area where the princess had thrown her jewelry. He had not noticed the princess, but she could see him and his movements. With curiosity, the princess hid behind the tree trunk to observe the young farmer. He looked at the ground and found hundreds of golden jewelry. The princess saw him jumping and dancing, and his face become as radiant as the sun. He glanced to either side before sprinting in one direction. He came back five minutes later with some more farmers, and all their faces glowed with joy. The princess looked through the eyes of those farmers, and a weird feeling settled within her. She felt warm inside, a beautiful, peaceful feeling, a calm state that she had never experienced before. The muscles of her face were tight and relaxed at the same time, drawing a pure smile.

She was happy.

HELP

Riiing, riiing...

"Hello?"

"¡Hola Mónica! ¿Cómo estás?"

"Excuse me? I am not Mónica, my name is Alice. Wrong number."

"Oh, I see... I am sorry to bother you."

"It's okay... Are you Spanish?"

"I am from Buenos Aires. I have been living here in the US since 2012. Right now settled in Boston."

"Okay, anyway..."

"This may sound a little awkward, but...I need help. My name is Carlos, by the way."

"I don't know you, I don't think I can help."

"I want to commit suicide. If you don't help me, you will be responsible for my death."

"What the fuck? No, I will not! What are you saying? I'm gonna hang up."

"Wait, Alice! This is your opportunity to do something right, finally."

"What do you mean with this 'finally'?"

"I'm a psychologist. From the way you answered me, I can relate that you are not very keen on helping people. And this is something that frustrates you."

"You know shit about me, okay? And why am I still talking to you?"

"Because you have the chance to help someone. Because

you are not the bad person you think you are, and you want to prove it to yourself."

"Okay. I'm gonna go along with your game. Why do you want to kill yourself?"

"I will answer your question later, but first, tell me something about you."

"About me? It's you who needs help. I'm not gonna explain shit."

"Well, if I want to trust you, I need to know who I'm talking with."

"Pfff... All right. My name is Alice, I am thirty-five years old. I live in a village called Danville, close to Lexington. I have lived here all my life. I work in a supermarket. I am divorced with three children. Now tell me, why are you thinking about committing suicide?"

"Why are you divorced?"

"My alcoholic ex-husband used to beat me from time to time. He left our home when I was pregnant with my younger daughter, and I never heard from him anymore...until two years ago, when I received a letter from a hospital in Cincinnati. The motherfucker was driving drunk when he crashed his car into a truck. He died immediately. The truck driver also died. Even in his last moments this asshole had to ruin someone else's life."

"You've had a hard life, haven't you?"

"Well...my father was an alcoholic too. He beat my mother too. It looks like we're following a pattern, like our life is already written when we're born."

"Interesting point. And why do you still live in the same village where you were born? Why don't you change your pattern?"

"Ah, it's complicated. I never really had the opportunity to leave. Of course, when you're a teenager, you have the idea to collect some money and leave this shit place behind. But it never happens, you know? Instead, you meet some random guy with his own car, you start dating him, he gets you pregnant, and in the blink of an eye, you're divorced with three children and living alone in a shitty apartment."

"I think you deserve something better."

"Well, I'm pretty good now. I have a stable job, my ex-husband is burning in hell, my children are doing good at school..."

"Do you have a pen and paper?"

"Yes, why?"

"Take them, and write down what I will say to you."

"Okay...ready."

"Boston, Harrison Ave, number 345, second floor. Ring the bell of the first floor, say you are coming to meet Carlos Monteagudo, they will let you in. Key is under the carpet. Move the fridge, behind it is a box. It is for you."

"What? What's inside the box? Why are you giving me something?"

"Inside the box, you will find two million dollars. I don't have any family to give it to, nor any good friends."

"What? Are you serious? And what about you?"

"I am serious. You are a good person. You deserve a better life. Use it."

Bang!

"Carlos? Carlos? Carlos!"

CALMANTIA

It all begun in 2023, with news that went initially unnoticed by most of the people but would change our world forever. "A new species of flower discovered in Ethiopia could have properties for healing anxiety and depression." They named it calmantia. It was a yellow flower with thick petals, similar to a tulip. It became popular firstly in para-pharmacies, mostly bought by vegans and naturopaths, and it quickly spread to the rest of the population. They began to sell it in botanic stores, then in supermarkets. Eventually, you could find it everywhere.

I remember the first time I tried it. I had been working the whole day, and I still needed to deliver three more reports by the end of the week. I had been exhausted and utterly stressed. I arrived home at 9 p.m. To my surprise, my wife had been waiting for me with a huge smile.

"How do you feel, honey?" she had asked me.

"I'm tired, close to death. The amount of work we've had recently is insane."

"Look what I bought."

She showed me a pot with calmantia. They looked pretty, with their shiny yellow petals, almost golden, and a thick, deep green stem. I didn't believe in the properties of the calmantia; I treated it as something that gets trendy for a moment and vanishes after a few months.

"Do you really believe that this flower does something?" I asked.

"Yes, of course. I already tried it."

She waved the flowers in front of my face.

"You just need to smell them."

I did. What did I have to lose? I inhaled deeply, bringing me a fragrance of a woody, earthy scent, kind of subtle.

"That's it?" I said. "I can't feel..."

All of a sudden, a peaceful feeling came inside me. From that moment, all my worries and problems looked insignificant and easy to solve. They had not changed: I still had to deliver three reports by the end of the week, my boss was still a dickhead, we still had to pay the credit of the small flat where we lived. But nothing seemed problematic anymore.

The next few days at work went well. I was more productive than ever, having abandoned the stress that I had before. The effect lasted about three days.

Calmantia became ultra-popular in two weeks. Initially, scientists recommended to be careful with it because they didn't know the side effects it could have. But very soon, they found out that the effect that calmantia had in our bodies was just caused by its smell, and there were no harming substances causing any kind of distress or addiction.

It was a complete boom. Every store wanted to sell calmantia, even supermarkets, gas stations, and furniture stores. It became a necessity, used by almost everybody.

The effects of calmantia lasted for about three days, in which you got rid of your anxieties, you were able to deal with your problems, and it awarded you with a very good mood. The petals of calmantia started to fall after two weeks, when the plant lost its effects and died after a few days.

Companies tried to make incense, pills, infusions, and all kinds of products with calmantia. But the only way that it would work was by smelling it directly from a live flower.

It became a massive produce. The plant grew better

in warm countries, so the huge plantations of cereals and rice from Africa, Asia, and South America were being progressively replaced by calmantia in order to feed the worldwide need of inhaling the earthy scent of the flower.

Everything changed after the emergence of calmantia. The economy grew, people were happier, technology and investigation led to finding the cure of some disease... It looked like we had found a way to push human brain function to one hundred percent.

2024 was said to have been the most productive and developing year of the history of humanity, thanks to calmantia. But in 2025, the debacle began. The worst world crisis since World War II. A plague of microscopic worms started to affect the calmantia plantations, making them unable to grow and die before flourishing. There were no pesticides working against the plague, as calmantia was so sensitive that it would not grow under the usage of any chemical products.

The calmantia producer countries, which were already affected by the lack of their basic aliments due to calmantia monoculture, collapsed. The sudden stop of calmantia exports brought poverty, poverty brought famine, and famine brought wars.

Most consumer countries began a spiral of depression and economic crisis that led to political changes and more restrictive laws and depletion of individual and collective freedom.

Calmantia became illegal worldwide in the summer of 2026, having left a burned field behind in our world, and was considered extinct six months later.

And what's happening now? Well... I can say that calmantia is not completely extinct. I found a way to grow calmantia in my garage. It started as a small calmantia plantation for my own usage and for my friends and family.

Soon, I started to make huge amounts of money. Now I have a big, clandestine farm of calmantia, which I sell to actors, athletes, businessmen, and politicians. And for myself, of course. It is the key to success.

BIRDS

I lost my job in the winter. To be honest, I was happy to be unemployed. I had worked so hard that I felt I needed rest. A couple of months dedicated to myself would not be bad until I got the next job. I would finally have time to practice yoga in the mornings, learn to bake cakes and, why not, read some gossip magazines that I hadn't had the chance to touch since I was twenty.

Jack came to the bed before leaving for work.

"Honey, will you be good?"

"Of course I will," I said.

"Text me if you need anything." He kissed me in the forehead.

I was alone in the apartment. *Where do I start?* I would maybe take a long shower, those that you can only afford when you have all the time in the world, and think about imaginary discussions with your high school archenemy or conversations you would have with that famous actor you liked very much. Later, I would go to the grocery store and do the laundry. Those were my obligations for the day. The rest was all mine.

I prepared a coffee and sat on the balcony. The winter sun touched the side of our living room during the mornings, and it warmed my skin so much that I was in my pajamas without the need of a sweater. I lit a cigarette. I didn't usually smoke, but I wanted to give myself a present. The fresh air went through my trousers and the sun warming my skin gave me goosebumps. I slid my hand down my belly, under my trousers. Between my legs, I was wet. I began to masturbate. I had not done it for a very long time, and it felt incredible. I didn't need to imagine anyone; just the picture of me touching myself on the balcony turned me on. I opened my eyes for a moment. There was a bird standing on the balustrade. It was a small gray bird, hopping on both legs and staring at me. It made me feel uncomfortable, like I was being observed, and I went back inside. I couldn't focus anymore so I left my sexual delight for later. I prepared a sandwich and went back to the balcony. The bird was still there, but it flew away when I opened the door.

I did the laundry, and I went back to the balcony to use the last moments of direct sun. I took a magazine I bought last week. An article of a girl caught on the street holding hands with a guy who was not her husband was the main theme. Boring. I lit another cigarette. It had been so long since I could do literally nothing, just sit and contemplate the park in front of our building. The winter left the trees barren, but the park still had an overall pale green color. The city didn't care much about that park, and on the grass, a bunch of wild weeds grew, making it an untamed area. On a tree, I noticed a bird standing. It was the same bird that visited me before on the balcony, or at least it looked like the same one to me. I called it Greytone.

The rest of the day was peaceful. I went to the grocery store, prepared lunch and not much more. When Jack came home, I was sitting in the living room in front of my laptop, pretending to be looking for job offers.

"Hi, honey. How was your day?" he asked.

"It was good. I was just looking for job offers. Nothing interesting."

"Don't worry about that, you will find something soon for sure."

I was totally not worried about that. I didn't wish to find a job soon. I wanted to enjoy my freedom for a while.

I developed some routines. I woke up early in the morning

at the same time as Jack. When he left, I sat on the balcony with a coffee, and I smoked a cigarette. It was the best time of the day. The morning sun, the view of the park, the calmness, and the almost forgotten feeling of being alone without any pressure... And the sound of the birds. I began to observe them, and I tried to identify them by colors and their singing. Greytones were easy ones; they were common, and their sound was familiar to me. Sometimes, one of them would come to the balcony while I was sitting and observed me like I observed it. Blackstones were bigger than Greytones and sang a precious melody that I could listen to for hours. I noticed they waited until other birds stopped singing to start their chirp. Birds were far more polite than humans. We were always eager to talk and we gave the sound going out of our own mouths too much importance. People loved to listen to themselves, but they didn't want to hear what others had to say.

The weeks passed, and I developed my skills in finding birds – it became my obsession. I bought binoculars to observe them better. I looked like I was stalking our neighbors. I could spend hours just trying to catch them and follow their movements. Some of them left and others came with the arrival of good weather. They flew thousands of kilometers every year to live in the perfect temperature for them. They wouldn't stay in a place they didn't like. I didn't like this city, for example. Well, I liked it in the summer, but not in the winter. I could also fly away and go to a warmer country in the winter and come back in the summer. Why not? I didn't have a job anyway. And I didn't want to work at the moment either.

One sunny spring morning, while I was observing a couple of Redwings, I had a weird feeling on my arm, like something scratched my skin from the sleeves of my shirt. I took off my shirt, and I noticed a small gray patch on my skin, like a tiny furry spot. I thought it was just a little bit of dust, so I put my shirt on again.

The next day, I had the same kind of feeling in my other arm and my back. I thought I got scabies or something like that, but I didn't want to visit a doctor. I felt hungry, and I wanted nuts or something hard and salty on a whim. I went to the grocery store, and I bought a big bag of sunflower seeds. I had never bought sunflower seeds before, and they were delicious. That wooden flavor and the hard skin breaking between my teeth was incredible. Why had I never bought them? I ate the whole bag.

The itching on my skin was annoying me, and now I had it all over my back as well. I went to the bathroom to check if I had any bump or rash. I was shocked. My whole body was covered by a smooth gray fur. I looked closer. They looked like small feathers, those that small chicks had. I got scared at the beginning, but surprisingly, I didn't give it much weight. I continued doing my things.

When Jack came home that evening, I wore a t-shirt that made visible all my small feathers.

"Honey, I'm a little worried about you," he said. I didn't know how I would explain the sudden rise of feathers on my skin. I had no idea what was going on either.

"Why?" I pretended I didn't know what he was talking about.

"You've been looking for a job for almost three months, and you haven't gotten any. This is not important, but I think you are spending too much time at home without doing anything. You could sign up for some activities, a gym, a lecture club..."

"What? What are you talking about? What about my skin?"

"What do you mean? What happened to your skin?"

I couldn't believe he hadn't seen my feathers. I ran into our room and closed the door. I observed myself in the mirror. My skin was covered with feathers, and they were bigger compared to when I first saw them in the morning. The pale gray color had changed to a darker carbon gray, and some of them started to get a beautiful orange color. For the first time, I enjoyed looking at them, and I admired myself in front of the mirror. I opened my arms, and I turned and jumped across the room, contemplating how the feathers danced with my movements. Good that Jack didn't come to the room at this time, because he would think I went crazy.

The next morning, Jack left our flat without saying a word. It was okay for me; he was probably still shocked about my feathers, and he needed some time to accept it. I decided to embrace the new me. Me with feathers. I noticed that more birds than ever came to visit me on the balcony, maybe attracted by the sunflower seeds I ate the day before, or just curious about the big bird they had in front.

Jack didn't come home to the flat alone. Jessica, my friend from childhood, was with him.

"Hi, honey! Look who came with me."

"Hello, Jessica! What are you doing here?" I asked.

"We haven't seen each other in a long time. Jack texted me and asked if I could come."

"You could have also texted me," I said.

"Honey..." Jack looked more serious. "I'm worried about you. We are worried about you. You're spending the whole day at home on the balcony without doing anything. I'm not saying you should look for a job, but at least go out, do a course, swim..."

"You could come with me to yoga," said Jessica. "I go in the mornings..."

"What are you talking about?" I said. "What about my skin? You're saying this because you don't accept me like I am!" I took off my T-shirt to show my beautiful feathers, and I moved my arms up and down to make them shine.

"Honey, please!" Jack looked angry. "Stop with this!

Dress yourself!"

"What happened to your skin?" Jessica tried to sound calm, but I could see that she was confused.

"Come, Jessica," said Jack, "I'll drive you home."

They left me in the living room alone. I heard Jack thanking Jessica for coming. I didn't understand why she had to come. And I couldn't believe they didn't comment on my feathers.

I went out to the balcony. The twilight left pink traces in the sky, which reflected beautifully on my shiny gray and orange feathers. I reclined on the balustrade and put first one leg over and then the other, holding the railing with one hand. The view of the park was astonishing, the green already returning with spring. Some trees were flourishing, and the birds flew in groups, playing and flirting, celebrating the longer days. I looked up at the sky, and in a brief moment of courage, I jumped to fly. To fly away. And I never came back.

BODY

I open my eyes. What is this terrible headache? My whole body hurts, and I can't remember what I did yesterday. This place doesn't sound familiar to me. What the fuck? There is a girl lying on the floor. Is she sleeping? Wait...she's dead! Fuck. The floor of this kitchen is covered in blood. My hands are also smeared with blood. Did I kill her?

Ding-dong, ding-dong. Someone is ringing the bell.

"Police, open the door!"

I have to get out of here, right now. There is a window in the bathroom that leads to a small alley. I look down, it's a second floor. I can jump. One, two, three! I have pain in my legs, but I guess I didn't get injured. Where to go now? I put my hands in my pockets: phone, wallet...and there is a card of a club, *The Golden Gate.* I will follow the only clue that I have right now.

I can't get the image of the girl lying dead on the floor out of my head. Why can't I remember anything? Why is this happening to me? I am just a simple journalist.

On my way to the Golden Gate, I pass through a small kiosk. On the front page of every main newspaper is a big picture of a girl and the word *Missing.* I get a closer look. *Veronica, the daughter of the governor, disappeared two days ago. The police have all personnel out in search of her.* Fuck. I'm in huge trouble.

The Golden Gate is a nightclub located in the outskirts of the city, a decrepit yellow building with some fake Ionic columns on the entrance with peeling paint and a huge parking lot in front. I'm sweating. I don't know if it's because of my walking speed or due to this torrid weather. The club is closed, but there is a waiter cleaning inside. He looks at me, waves and gives me a big smile. He seems to recognize me.

"Hey! It's you!" he says. "How's your hangover?"

"Good morning... Ehm, could you tell me if I was alone here yesterday?"

"Alone? You mean, alone with that pretty girl? It looked like you both had a good connection. Did the night end well?" He winks. It disgusts me.

The TV is on. On the news, they are talking about Veronica's disappearance. The police already found the body. The waiter focuses on the TV for a few seconds.

"Wait a moment... This girl looks so similar to your girl."

"I have to go."

I really have to go before he calls the police. I rush out of the place. According to what the waiter said, I was here yesterday with Veronica. And apparently, we knew each other. As reported in the newspapers, Veronica disappeared two days ago. How long were we together?

Something vibrates in my pocket. This is not my phone. I should pick up anyway, I will just keep silent. A male voice talks without letting me speak. "Veronica? Are you all right? Let's meet at four o'clock at Boulevard Station. Hurry up please, honey."

I hang up. I have two hours to get there to meet this guy.

Boulevard Station is not crowded at this hour. The glass ceiling lets the sunlight enter and warm the station like a greenhouse, producing a suffocating hotness. How can I find the guy? I decide to call the same number and check if someone from the platform answers the phone. I glance around, and I see a guy with a hippy look taking the phone from his jacket. He stares at me for a second, and he bolts in the opposite direction. I follow him. He runs faster, but I don't lose him. He turns into a corridor. I get there after a moment, but I can't see nobody. I feel a smash on the back of my head, and I fall on the floor. The hippy guy is just behind me, and he grabs my neck with both hands.

"Where is Veronica?"

I can't breathe. "She...she is...dead."

"You killed her!" he is choking me with all his strength.

My consciousness wavers. I kick him so that he falls. We start a wrestling fight until I am finally on him, and I have his arms blocked.

"I didn't kill her!" I shout.

I explain everything that happened to me since I woke up: the body, the police, my amnesia, the Golden Gate...

"My name is Arthur," he says. "Veronica was in danger, so I wanted to help her escape."

"Why was she in danger?"

"She is...was an activist, like me. Her father is letting Boilder Company dump waste in the port. Of course, he is getting huge amounts of money for it. Veronica and I were about to make it public when she received a message blackmailing her. I told her to let it go and move away, but she wanted to stick with her plan. She is very stubborn."

"That's probably why she contacted me. I'm a journalist for the *New Times* newspaper."

"Right. If you don't remember anything, it's possible that she drugged you with GHB so you would publish the information she had without you hesitating. That's why you don't remember anything."

We both got to our feet. My neck still hurts from his hands.

"Where should we go now?" I ask.

"Let's visit the governor. I think he might be involved."

"Do you think he would kill his own daughter?"

"He is capable of this and much more."

The house of the governor is in a residential area away from the crowds of the city, surrounded by greenery and villas with huge gardens. I follow Arthur; it looks like he has been here before.

"I know how to sneak into the house," he says. "I visited Veronica during the night for a long time."

We go through the back of the house and jump the fence. I feel like a criminal. On the way to the house, I notice some policemen going around the neighborhood, and now I am sneaking into the governor's house with a hippy that I just met. It could be a trap, but I have already gone too far. We hide in the bushes. The evening light lets us see two silhouettes stepping in our direction. They stop just a few meters from us. My heart wants to get out of my chest, and I struggle to keep my breaths quiet.

"It's safe to talk here, officer. There are no security cameras," says one of the men.

"All right, Governor. The job is almost done. We just need to find her friend Arthur and that journalist. We will charge them with the murder of Veronica. It won't be difficult as her body was in Arthur's flat."

"Good job, but find them quickly. I want to get rid of this problem as soon as possible. And remember, nobody knows this except you and me."

I glance at Arthur. He has tears on his cheeks, and his face is red. His breath is quick and deep. He has in front of him the two people who are in charge of the murder of his lover, and they talk about it like they would talk about buying tomatoes in the market.

Arthur stands and hustles toward them. He puts a hand in his pocket and takes out a gun. He aims at the governor and shoots him three times. He twists and shoots the officer three times. He faces the governor again, shooting him four more times in the face, yelling like a man possessed. The police appear in a few seconds, and an avalanche of gunfire reaches Arthur. I move away from the scene as quick as I can. A police officer finds me in the garden.

"Hey, you! Stop!" He points at me with his gun. "What are you doing here?"

"I'm a journalist. I just heard some gunfire, and I came here." I show him my journalist card, shaking.

"Get away from here right now!"

No need to tell me twice. I move out of the garden and head to my apartment as fast as I can. When I arrive, I turn on the TV.

"Veronica's murderer, Arthur Doyle, fell dead in an encounter with the police, after having killed the governor and a police officer." They assert that Arthur had mental issues and that he had been harassing Veronica for a long time.

I'm exhausted. I go to bed and open my laptop. I received an e-mail from Veronica. She sent me all the information about the contracts that his father had under the table with Boilder Company. Should I publish them? I will think about it tomorrow.

WAR

Ahmed heard a loud shot and immediately lay on the ground. He looked back and noticed that Bill was on the floor with his head facing the mud.

"Fuck! Bill, are you okay? Bill? Bill?"

Ahmed crawled next to Bill, trying to wake him up. Bill had a bullet in his chest. Blood flowed, red and warm, and Bill's eyes had a lost look. He was dead. Ahmed took a quick glance at his surroundings, he couldn't see anything more than a deep forest covered by a dense fog. He knew he had very few chances to survive. Bill was the last man standing from his troop; all the other eight companions had faced the same fate.

Ahmed stood quickly and dashed in a random direction. He had no hope, he was just waiting to hear the bang that would mean the end of his life. And the end of the war for him. He sprinted for fifteen minutes in a straight line. Nobody shot him. *Not yet*, he thought. He was exhausted, but there was no time to rest.

After five hours of walking, he left the forest behind him and found a blue lake surrounded by green fields. Two hours had passed since he last heard the sound of a bullet or explosion. He felt safe, as he had not felt during the last three weeks. Two hundred meters from where he stood, just next to the lake, there was a small wooden hut. He approached, willing to find someone who could help him and give him some food. There was nobody inside. There was just a small blanket, a pot, some wood and some fruit that was still edible. Probably the owner found himself forced to leave quickly to escape the war. *I would escape too*, thought Ahmed.

He took some fruits, sat outside the hut, and cried. How he could have known what the war was about? What was the sense of it? During the last two months since he enrolled in the army, he had seen friends die and innocents be murdered. He had faced death. He had spent infinite nights awake waiting for an enemy attack, shaking, scared. His superiors were persistent in trying to make the soldiers hate the enemy. It didn't work with Ahmed. He was reminded of the first man he killed and how terrible he had felt. He could just keep thinking about who this person was that he shot, if he had family, what he left behind. He remembered how he tried to hide the tears that flowed down his face while his companions congratulated him and patted him on the shoulder. The war was cruel and pointless.

Ahmed went back inside the hut and covered himself with a blanket. He was tired, and his eyelids were drooping. Out of the blue, he was underwater, unable to breathe. He tried so hard to swim to the surface, to escape, but it was impossible to reach. Bill was also in the water, his heart losing blood. Bill was trying to talk to him underwater, bubbling something that seemed like, "Help me."

"I can't help you, Bill."

Ahmed opened his eyes, sweating, his heart beating like a machine gun. He struggled to fall asleep again, making an effort to wipe out from his head the image of Bill's inert body.

The next day, he woke up early. The sun shone like he had not seen since he was in the war. He felt better than the day before, even though he knew that it was a matter of time before either the enemy or his own army would find him. And both options were equally terrible: if the enemy found him, they would kill him immediately. If his army found him, he would be accused of treason for abandoning the war. In the best case scenario, he would be judged, and then he would be executed. He remembered how Lieutenant McMathew executed one soldier in front of his platoon because he wanted to desert. The lieutenant was cruel, one of the worst people he had ever met. He enjoyed the war the same way a child loved sweets, and he was delighted with death, cruelty, and authority.

Ahmed took his handgun and went for a stroll next to the lake. With every small sound he heard, he turned around, alert. It didn't matter if it was an animal moving or the breeze. The war had changed him, made him suspicious, scared and unable to relax. He almost didn't remember his village, his family, or his home. The time during the war looked so long and the days were infinite. He recalled his first day in the army when he met his platoon, and he was so excited about going to the front. Then came his first battle, when the excitement quickly turned into fear as he heard the blasts and the smell of gunpowder and the view of his first companion dying next to him.

It started to rain, he came back to the hut, and he lay on the blanket. A cat came in meowing, it looked very friendly. The cat approached Ahmed, and the closer it got, the bigger it became, until it turned into a big tiger with a salivating mouth. Ahmed tried to escape, but his body didn't react, and he couldn't move a muscle. The tiger jumped on Ahmed, opening its threatening jaw.

Ahmed opened his eyes. It was already night.

The days were passing, and the fear of being caught by the army was slowly being replaced for comfort and ease. Ahmed started to enjoy the calmness of the place and the warm and humidity of the days of summer. He designed a method for fishing with a nail and a string. His diet consisted basically of fish, vegetables, and fruits that he collected. He spent hours walking around the lake, appreciating the peaceful routine he made. The hardest part was still the night, when he had constant nightmares of finding himself trapped and unable to escape. But he enjoyed the rest of the day and started to feel a brief happiness like he had not had in a long time. He was forgetting about the war.

He had not seen a single person since Bill was killed. He continuously wondered if he was really alive or this place was a kind of heaven. He questioned himself about everything. He doubted his religion, he thought and rethought his convictions and beliefs. Nothing from his past made sense anymore; he would change a lot of things from his previous life if he went back home. But now he didn't want to go back home anymore.

The peaceful and calm days came to an end. One day, in the early morning when Ahmed was fishing, he heard some voices coming from afar. There were some soldiers marching in his direction. He couldn't see if they were from his own army or from the enemy. He didn't feel scared or sad. He rested, calm and peaceful, and kept fishing. He didn't fear death.

They stood next to Ahmed. Their faces looked empty and exhausted, as if they had been walking through the desert without water for forty days. He recognized the uniforms from his army. In front of eight soldiers stood Lieutenant McMathew.

"Good morning, soldier," said Lieutenant McMathew. "What are you doing here? From which company are you?"

"Good morning, Lieutenant. I am from the forty-fourth company. All my companions died in the war."

"The war is over. We won. You must come with us now. Later on, you will have a trial for deserting."

"I am not coming with you. I am staying here," said Ahmed.

The eyes of the lieutenant burned with pure hate. The other soldiers peered at Ahmed with a face of empathy and pity.

"Your company disappeared. Nobody knows you're here. If you don't come with us, I am going to execute you right now!" shouted Lieutenant McMathew.

"Lieutenant, you are a horrible person," said Ahmed. "You feed yourself with hate. The world would be a better place without people like you."

The lieutenant aimed at Ahmed with his handgun.

"I am going to kill you!"

A loud shot made Ahmed shut his eyes for a brief moment that felt like it lasted a year. He didn't feel anything. When he opened his eyes, he saw the lieutenant falling dead on the ground. A soldier had aimed at him from the back, still shaking and face pale.

"Ahmed, nobody knows you're here," said the soldier. "We're going back home, but you can stay. The war changed all of us, some for good like you, and some for bad like me. I hope you have a good life."

Ahmed nodded. He continued fishing while the soldiers walked away. The body of the lieutenant lay on the ground right next to him. He didn't bother.

CHASE

Again the same noise. Something scratched the roof, moved around and moaned, stomping and making the lamps shake as if a tropical typhoon would pass through the house... John was awake one more time, lying on the bed staring at the ceiling. It was the fourth night in a row that he was unable to sleep, and he was enraged.

John had never had a good temper, always groaning and complaining, being angry at the world and his surroundings. He never accepted having been taken away from Vietnam, and he always considered that his nation acted cowardly. He had the same opinion about his platoon, to whom he referred as a bunch of wimp namby-pamby flower-eater hippies.

The night initiated in the same way as the three previous ones. John went to sleep at 2200 hours after his ritual of tidying up himself, drinking a glass of warm water, and praying. After about one hour of being in bed, the fuss started. Firstly, small steps treading on the wooden housetop, as if something was moving cautiously to not get caught. The quiet ramble was followed later by a din of three hours of crashes, blasts, and bawls. *This needs to stop*, thought John.

Next morning, with his eyes half-closed with sleeplessness, John drove his pick-up Ford Super Duty to the hardware store.

"I need something to get rid of an animal that is making trouble during the night under my roof," he said to a Latino employee.

"Good morning, sir. Which kind of animal are we talking about?"

"I don't know, I haven't seen it. Does it really matter? He's just fucking around all night, and I want to get rid of it."

"Well, yes it matters, sir. We have different kinds of traps to-"

"Shut up, tacohead!" John interrupted. "Just give me the deadliest trap you have."

"Sir, please, a little bit of respect. I am not even Mexican. I am from Cuba."

"Same, same."

The store employee gave John a couple of box traps.

"Those should work for different kind of animals: raccoons, gophers, skunks, cats, opossums... You just need to put some bait inside and wait until the animal is trapped. Then, you release it into the wild."

"Okay, thank you, beaner."

"See you, old fart."

John walked away carrying the two box traps on his right shoulder and raised his left hand to show his middle finger to the employee.

Once at home, he climbed to the attic to place both boxes. He put all kinds of food inside them: beef, peanuts, cheese, and celery. He didn't have the intention of releasing the animal once it was captured. Instead, he would kill it.

He spent the day sitting on his porch, drinking cold beer and contemplating the street. A group of multiracial kids played with a ball in front of his house, to which John reacted with a grimace of disgust. The ball accidentally reached his porch. John took the knife he had on the table and punctured the ball, smirking at the kids who went back, dejected, to their houses.

John had been living in the same place since he was born, and he observed how the neighborhood had transformed through the years. When he was a child, it was mostly formed by families of workers looking for the American dream of owning a detached house with its own backyard. With time, almost all the neighbors moved to different areas, and the houses were now inhabited by Asians, Latinos and black people, which made John feel like a stranger in his home.

The night finally came, and John prepared to go to sleep after having washed himself, drank a glass of warm water, and prayed. He stayed awake until the noise started. Like the previous days, it began as timid steps on the wood followed by loud blasts. Suddenly, the noise stopped completely. *I got you!* he thought. He fell asleep immediately for the first time in the last five nights.

He didn't need an alarm clock in order to wake up the next morning. He jumped from the bed and ran up to the attic. He was eager to know which kind of animal had been bothering him the last few days and take his revenge. He was stunned when he got upstairs. "Motherfucker!" he shouted. Both boxes were empty, and there was no trace of the bait inside.

John was furious. *I didn't kill dozens of dinks in Vietnam to be fooled by a fucking animal in my own house!* He was also mad at the guy who sold him the box traps, assuming that he tricked him and cursing globalism for leading the white Americans to slowly lose their rights.

He threw away the box traps and prepared to deal with the animal by himself. He went to the gun shop to buy some bullets. He dragged a big trunk up to the attic, with which he built a fort for hiding himself. He took an old military jacket he had from the war, charged his old M-14 assault rifle, and he left some food in the middle of the attic. It took him a whole day to set up everything.

The night came, and John was thrilled. He waited behind the trunk, dressed as an old veteran war soldier trying to remind himself of his glorious days, aiming at the bait he left with his rifle waiting for his prey. He couldn't remember the last time he felt as young and enthusiastic.

The wait seemed endless, and John started to feel a pressure in his bladder because of his prostate hypertrophy. He needed to pee so badly. He grabbed an empty jar he had next to him and released his physiological needs. Right in that moment, he heard some soft footsteps getting closer. John left what he was doing and gripped his rifle, pointing aimlessly, still with his pants unbuttoned.

Finally, he saw it. It was a simple raccoon, lurching in a quest for food. He aimed at the raccoon, who was unaware of the menace, ready for shooting. *I got you.* John fired the gun. But he forgot about the recoil. He bounced away two meters, crashing into the wall and leaving a huge cramp on his shoulder and pain in his back, making him almost unable to move. The raccoon, far from getting panicked, glanced at John with disregard and proceeded to taste the food he had prepared leisurely. John was too dazed to react, and he could only lean, watching how the raccoon enjoyed the meal, exasperated by his defeat.

The next day, he could barely walk. *Today, I am finishing you, even if it's the last thing I do!* He limped to the attic and prepared some homemade traps with nets and ropes. He cleaned his arsenal of guns and rifles and put them in a line, ready to use them. He wanted to kill the raccoon at all costs. *Enough of this humiliation!* John felt empowered and prepared for the attack. Waiting in his improvised fort, armed up to the teeth, he fantasized about pulling the trigger. The raccoon showed up as usual. It quickly minced to the bait and started his private feast. John aimed at the raccoon, this time with a handgun, a small revolver Smith 442. He shot. To his surprise, the raccoon remained next to the food, staring at him impassively. He had missed the shot. John stood up and dashed closer to the raccoon.

"Aren't you afraid of me?" he shouted, pointing at the animal with his gun.

The raccoon peered at John while chewing the food. Then, it moved to John and stroked his leg.

"What are you doing? I am going to kill you!"

The raccoon ignored John's threat and kept rubbing itself on John's legs, its eyes firmly fixed on his face. John felt something inside, a sort of kindness and compassion. He felt as if the raccoon was thanking him for the meals.

"Oh, you are hungry, aren't you?" said John, leaving his revolver on the floor. "Take it, eat your dinner."

John named the raccoon Charlie, the same name that the American forces used to call the North Vietnamese soldiers. He prepared a meal for the raccoon every evening and left it in the attic as a part of his night ritual.

One summer afternoon, John was sitting on his porch drinking cold beer and contemplating the street. A group of multiracial kids were playing with a ball in front of his house. The ball fell accidentally on John's porch. The kids looked at him, frightened. John stood from his chair, took the ball, and threw it back to the kids, drawing a subtle smile on his mouth.

ABOUT THE AUTHOR

Ferran Plana was born in 1988, at present settled in Barcelona. He began his writing passion after a long period of improvising bedtime stories for his wife before sleeping. When he is not writing, you might find him building a sand castle on the beach, observing birds with his binoculars, playing cello or trombone, or in the hospital working as a doctor. *The Fabric Over The Moon* is his first published short story and flash fiction collection.

Find more about him at: www.ferranplanabooks.com

AUTHOR'S NOTE

Dear reader,

Thank you for reading *The Fabric Over The Moon*. I hope you enjoyed reading this book as much as I did writing it. If you liked the book (or even if you didn't), please consider writing a short review in Amazon. This will bring a great feedback for me, and will help other readers find stories similar to *The Fabric Over The Moon*. For future publications and news, please visit my website: www.ferranplanabooks.com

Made in United States
North Haven, CT
14 June 2025

69794119R00092